Ursula Spark
and the
Fourth Frankenstein

Cole Smith

**COLE
SMITH
WRITES**

Ursula Spark and the Fourth Frankenstein

Copyright 2019 by Cole Smith. All rights reserved.
Printed in the United States. For more information, contact
cole@colesmithwrites.com

Summary: Ursula Spark and her friends try to find a thief's
identity after a robbery
occurs during a viewing of the 1931 *Frankenstein* film.

ISBN: 978-1-7321202-3-5
[Teen and Young Adult Fiction]

Book design by Cole Smith Writes.
Frankenstein cover illustration by Joseph Tisdale.

https://www.colesmithwrites.com

For my students and my teachers.

Acknowledgments

A book is never a solo project, and this one is no exception. Thank you to the Office of Letters and Light for hosting NaNoWriMo every year. It was a particularly rainy November when I first met Ursula and her friends, and NaNoWriMo gave me the courage to follow them.

Thank you to the founders, staff, and families of Parkersburg Christian School, who first nurtured my writing, and then gave me space and inspiration to see where it leads. It's a humbling honor to be a part of this ministry, and " … I thank my God upon every remembrance of you … "

Grateful thanks to Diane Tarantini, who edited, advised, and coached. Your friendship and professional guidance enrich and encourage me every week!

Bless everyone who volunteered to be beta readers and who suggested changes and tweaks that strengthened the weak spots. Your feedback is invaluable. Heather, Jill, and PJ—you're the best!

I've been privileged to mentor a number of students over the years who have been gifted with dyslexia. Their courageous determination, as well as the breath-taking talents they've displayed, have been an inspiration to me. Although dyslexia can bring struggle and heartache, it deals generously in creativity, problem-solving, and resilience. Many have gone on to do community-changing work, and I'm so proud. Thank you for not quitting.

I owe deep thanks to my critique groups, the Contemporary Writer's Group, and Third Saturday Writers. I still feel so lucky to be a member. You help me trim the excess and find the gold. And you have an uncanny way of knowing when I need affirmations and when I need to get to the point.

To my family who ask what I'm up to, then listen patiently as I describe .mobi files, social media platform-building, and miscellaneous writing projects: thanks for putting up with me!

To my husband who tiptoes through the house during writing time, who reminds me to take breaks, and who graciously shares our time with all the characters that live in my head: thank you, sweetheart! Now we can take more bike rides.

Above all, I want to thank our Creator, the great Author, who teaches us in stories and who calls us to create our own.

Chapter One

I'm the weird one.

It's because my brain works differently. My weird, dyslexic brain.

When I was in first grade, I *hated* my name. Imagine how hard it is to spell 'Ursula' when you have a brain as weird as mine. I'll never forget when my teacher took me to another room and asked me to read the word she wrote on the chalkboard. I told her I couldn't. It was Ursula. That's how I found out I was weird.

It's safe to say that school has never been my strong point. And if my school problems were the only things that made me weird, I'd really hate dyslexia even though Mom and Dad always told me I'd be glad for it one day. They said God knew what He was doing when he made my brain. Sometimes it was hard to believe, especially when I studied really hard but only made a so-so grade on a test.

Luckily, though, I'm *all* kinds of weird. For one thing, I can draw. In fact, if I could, I'd draw all day long. But, you know. School.

I can also see connections between random people and events.

That one, I discovered accidentally when I was little. When I was in third or fourth grade, my parents would get mad at me for spoiling the plots of tv shows we watched as a family. I could figure out what was going to happen, and I'd blurt it out. Finally, they made me promise to keep the answer to myself or else they'd stop watching tv with me. I promised.

One of the other things that makes me weird is how I like to smell the weather. My friends think it's bananas. But I don't care. When I'm by myself, I stick my nose in the air and sniff like a dog. And you know what? I can always smell when it's going to rain before anyone else. I won't lie, I always feel kind of smug when I can get out my umbrella and open it up moments before the rain starts.

In my opinion, October smells the best. It's one of my favorite months. And this was a day to remember.

I kicked the leaves off the sidewalk, turning my face to the warm, spotty sunlight shining through the row of sycamores. Closing my eyes, I inhaled autumn. It smelled like peppery dry leaves, a hint of wood smoke and the last sweet perfume of the nearby hay fields drying in the sun.

I leaped up the five concrete steps and buzzed the doorbell at Kaia's house. Kollin came to the door. He had a chocolate milk mustache framing his mouth, and his feathery hair was cow-licked in its usual way. He smiled when he saw me and my heart squiggled. I love that kid. Then he ran toward the heart of the house, one sock flapping crazily as he cornered. He wasn't allowed to let anyone in, even me, so I waited.

Finally Kaia appeared, looking as put-together as always, her creamy, almond-colored skin glowing, her dark curls bouncing a little as she approached. I willed my hand to stay at my side instead of creeping up to check my own messy, cropped bob. I waved through the glass storm door. Kaia waved back and

2

stepped onto the porch. She called over her shoulder, "We're leaving!"

Kaia's mom appeared from the kitchen. "Hi, Ursula!"

"Hello!"

"Eleven, right?" She hugged Kaia first, then me. She stepped back into the house but held the door open. Behind her, I could see Kollin galloping from the kitchen to the hall, dragging the baby on a quilt like a sled. I jabbed a finger over her shoulder, and she glanced at her sons. "Eleven," she repeated, nodding once before letting the door fall shut and turning to chase them.

I laughed and hitched my tote higher onto my shoulder. "Sure you don't want to hang around here for a little while?"

Kaia rolled her eyes. "I'm sure. Where's Livvie?"

"She's late, so she said she'll meet us there." We walked side-by-side down the sidewalk, and I kicked the leaves again. They were so dry and light, how could I help it? It was as good as popping bubble wrap.

Kaia checked her watch. "Are you sure she wasn't scared? What are the chances she'll actually make it?"

I made the so-so sign. "I think this is just her usual sort of late. Hopefully she'll show."

"Mmm," was all she said, and we walked the rest of the way to the Butler Theater in easy quiet—except for the leaf-crunching. That was one of my favorite things about Kaia. We could think together. Just think. And it was never awkward.

The line at the door wasn't too long, with only a few people standing around. But after we took our places in line, more and more people came, in groups of twos and threes. I gazed up at the marquee, and a lovely chill ran through me. FRANKENSTEIN, it read, in all capital letters.

Then the ambulance parked in front of the entrance.

"What happened?" I craned my neck and scanned the line, now

3

stretching around the corner. "Must be someone inside. I hope they're okay."

Kaia shook her head and leaned closer. "I read in the paper..."

She was always saying things like that. She was the only fifteen-year-old I knew who was caught up on local and national news, and several global crises.

"I read in the paper," she said, "that when this movie was shown for the first time—in the '30s, I think—it was so scary the hospital sent an ambulance to respond faster to anyone who might have a heart attack." She frowned. "It could have all been advertising. But people were really scared by stuff like this back then. So the article said that there would be an ambulance here tonight, to recreate the first showing. A couple of EMTs, too."

"Yikes," I murmured.

"Especially if it gets called out. Hope the county didn't have to pay for an extra ambulance for this." She narrowed her eyes, talking to herself, now. "No way, right?"

"What is *that*?!" Livvie's voice was shrill. She drew up alongside us on the sidewalk, clutching her bag with one hand and pointing in horror with the other. She turned to the older couple in line behind us. "Hi. Do you mind if I jump in line with my friends? They have my ticket already."

The lady seemed amused. "We have ours already, too. Go right ahead."

Livvie thanked them and shimmied close to me, quivering with nervousness. "Oh, my gosh, you guys, what happened? Why is there an ambulance here?"

I hugged her arm while Kaia repeated what she'd learned from the article. Livvie pranced like a tense pony, picking at her crimson fingernails. "You've got to be kidding me. I don't know why I let you guys convince me to come to this thing."

"It's not even going to be scary; it'll be funny," I said. "You

4

know how funny the special effects are going to look compared to movies now?"

"And," Kaia pointed out, "you love coming to the Butler Theater."

"Who doesn't? It's amazing."

I noticed the woman behind us suppressed a smile. Eavesdropper. How could I blame her, though? The line was getting boring. And we weren't exactly quiet.

An usher unlocked and propped open the door, greeting ticket holders and directing others to the sales booth. Kaia drew her ticket from her purse, and I pulled two tickets from my pocket and handed one to Livvie. We showed them to the usher and he waved us inside. At the top of several red-carpeted stairs was another usher, and he motioned for our tickets, then noticed Kaia. "You know your way around, don't you?" he asked, and gave us a toothy grin.

"I do," she said, and nodded toward the balcony stairwell. She was at the theater at least once a week. As we started up the winding wrought iron stairs, Livvie squealed.

I prodded her in the back with my sketchbook. "Keep going. You've got this."

"You guys, you have to go without me," she said, panting. Kaia and I exchanged a glance. It was hard to say how scared Livvie actually was, and how much of this was, itself, a performance. She did have a flair for the dramatic.

As we reached the top, a costumed Frankenstein turned and shuffled toward us from the dimly lit corridor. Livvie squealed again. "Oh, no!" She dove behind Kaia, who put her arm out to block the creature.

I tried to laugh, but truthfully the monster was freaking me out, too. "Hey," I said, faking bravery. "Cute boots!"

Kaia burst out laughing, and I felt better. She had Liv by the arm, and was trying to drag her up the last two steps. "Yeah, where'd you find those, Frankie?"

The thing raised its arms and followed his hands away from us, toward the other balcony stairwell. I let out my breath in a whoosh. The masked face was truly horrible. I watched him shuffle away. Who was in that costume? Turning to Kaia, I asked, "Someone you know?"

She had been a member of the stage crew for the Butler's production of an Agatha Christie mystery last month. In fact, she'd been involved with the theater ever since she'd joined the Butler's youth program a few years ago. It still surprised me that Kaia was such a killer actor. She was usually so straight-forward, so matter-of-fact.

She shook her head. "Who knows?" Her left eyebrow lifted. "If it is, I hope he'll reveal his identity before we leave."

Livvie gripped the doorway. "Can we just go sit down, please?"

We found our row at the front of the balcony and sank into the plush hinged seats. They groaned with the history of decades of performances. I tilted my head back to study the vaulted decorative ceiling. Ornamental golden frames encircled images of characters I didn't know. Greek ladies, and men dressed like centurions. A giant chandelier sparkled far above our heads.

Kaia followed my gaze. "I wonder how they dust that light?"

I glanced at her. "Is that all you can think of when you look up there? Dust?"

The corner of Kaia's mouth curled up, but she didn't answer. I flipped open my sketchbook and pulled my favorite pen from my tote. It was a Pentel EnerGel liquid gel ink pen. When our local drugstore quit selling them, I petitioned the store manager to bring them back. It didn't work, so now I had to order them online and stockpile them in my desk drawer at home. When someone asks me if they can borrow a pen, and the EnerGel is the only one with me, I have a moral crisis. Seriously, no one appreciates how important pens are, and how hard it is to find the right one.

I made a few quick lines, just to put down the bare-bones of the shapes and angles of the ceiling, the way the chandelier hung, the perspective from my seat. When I peered up again, Livvie was leaning across Kaia, her eyes fixed on my paper. "I love to watch you draw," she said, visibly calmer. "I wish I could draw like you can."

I capped the pen and flipped to a clean page. "Whenever you want to learn, you know I'll teach you."

She wrinkled her nose and swiped a stray curl from her forehead. "You always say that."

"It's true."

She shook her head and leaned back into her own seat, letting Kaia breathe. "You don't know how *awful* I am at art. I'm awful at everything."

Kaia pursed her lips.

"Liv," I said, "you're, like, the most talented person we know."

She flushed with pleasure. "Right ... That means a lot coming from Einstein and Picasso."

It didn't matter how many times we told her, Livvie never believed anything good about herself. She wasn't able to see what was obvious to everyone else. Truthfully, I was on the edge of panic about it. Her highs were very high, and her lows were super low. No one at school seemed to see how fragile she was, except me. Kaia could tell, though. I prayed for Liv every day, that she could recognize how great she was. In a way, it was a prayer for me, too, since I was tired of worrying about her.

The lights dimmed, and the buzz of the audience swelled, then faded.

"Oh, my goodness. Oh, my goodness. God, help me," Livvie

chanted.

Kaia leaned over and whispered, "You're freaking yourself out. Relax. Deep breaths."

When the title scene rolled, and the tuxedoed guy stepped out from behind the curtain to offer "… just a word of friendly warning," Liv's fretting had sunk to a low whimper. As the movie marched forward, I twisted in my seat to look at the rows of lit-up faces behind us. I always loved how mesmerized movie goers look. I think it's because they let their feelings ride along with the story. Everyone's in the same boat, on the same wave, for an hour and a half or so. I wanted to take a mental picture of their illuminated faces and tuck it away in my memory. Click.

As we watched, I felt kind of sorry for the monster. There were a lot of times I felt like I'd been created with the wrong brain, too. Poor guy.

A little while into the movie, when even Livvie had settled comfortably into the plot, Kaia leaned close to me and whispered, "Look." She flicked a finger toward the balcony entrance.

Frankie had reappeared, and was quietly stumping our way. I cringed. "Better warn Liv."

She nodded and whispered something to Livvie, who moaned and whipped her head around to watch him approach. "Oh, no! Go away!"

The people around us whisper-giggled. I couldn't help grinning as I uncapped my pen. A few quick lines, and I sketched Frankie's shoulders, the top of his head, the bend of his nearest arm, the heads of the audience and the backs of the seats. A murmur rose from the floor of the house below us and I sat forward in my seat a little to peer down. There were other Frankensteins meandering through the audience there, too. "Three more monsters," I told Kaia and pointed.

Our Frankenstein had drawn up behind us, but when he heard

me tell Kaia about the others, his arms fell to his sides. "Three?" His voice was muffled by the rubber mask.

That's all it took. The spell was broken for Livvie. "That wasn't very monsterly," she pouted, the words tinged with judgment.

Kaia watched the Frankenstein with interest. He took a few quick, unmonsterly strides to the balcony railing and leaned over it, studying the house below. A scream ripped through the theater.

Chapter Two

The Frankenstein peeled his mask off by the rubber hair and spun around. He jogged to the stairwell and disappeared down it. Kaia and I, and several others, rushed to the railing and leaned over, trying to see in the murky light. As a crowd assembled around the middle rows, a movement near the stage caught my attention. Another Frankenstein was pushing through the exit. I grabbed Kaia's arm and pointed. "Where does that door go?"

Kaia followed my gaze. "The alley."

"Come on," I said, and we pushed our way up the aisle as politely as possible.

"Wait! Where are you going?" called Livvie.

But I didn't slow down. "The alley!" I said, over my shoulder.

We raced down the stairs and joined a throng of confused patrons in the lobby. Murmuring excuse-me's as we went, we got to the main entrance and followed a group onto the sidewalk. I turned to look for Kaia.

"This way," she called through the crowd, and we ran to the corner of the building.

The side lot was dark. There were no street lights for the rest of the block, and the back of the theater looked just as dark as the lot.

I didn't have time to explain my instincts. "Get ready. Where's Livvie?"

"She didn't come. Get ready for what?" Kaia whispered as we crept along the wall toward the corner.

"Anything." Holding my hands in blades, ready to karate chop the monster, I flung myself around the corner and into the dim yellow glow of the exit light.

There was no one. Kaia and I relaxed, and let out our breath in two puffs of steam. Kaia grinned. "Well?"

"Guess he got away. Look." I bent to pick up a rubber Frankenstein mask from the sidewalk, just beyond the ring of light, and held it out for Kaia to see.

We both yelped when the door burst open and a Frankenstein clomped onto the sidewalk. It was Frankie from the balcony. His mask was still pushed back onto his forehead, making him look like he had two heads. He looked at us, then up and down the alley. "What are you doing out here?" he asked, whipping his heads back and forth.

Kaia glanced at me. She didn't know the answer.

I shrugged. "I saw one of you guys running for this exit, just after the woman screamed. So I ..." I trailed off. *I what?* I was going to tackle a dude in a dark parking lot? I had no business back here, and we all knew it. I pointed at the mask in my hand. "What happened in there?"

He reached out and took the mask, then pulled off his own and studied them side by side, frowning.

"They're the same," I said, comparing them in the poor light. Light. So much depended on light. It was powerful: contrast, shadow, line and sharpness. It was art. And real life.

He lowered the masks and took a step back. "I think you should go inside now. This isn't the best place to be at night." His voice was flat. It wasn't a suggestion.

11

I saw Kaia's nostrils flare, and tried to will her to keep calm. Last summer, she had delivered a very respectful, ten-minute speech to a police officer who told us that we needed to be careful while we were walking in the park alone. Kaia gave him a detailed argument about civil liberties and individual freedoms. She believed we could hold our own. But I wasn't as sure, and didn't ever want to find out. "Yeah, let's go back inside. Obviously, there's no one out here anymore." I pulled her by the belt loop.

"We have to go around," he said, motioning for us to go first. "This door locks from the inside."

As we made our way back to the entrance, I had more time to notice the parking lot, the length of the building, and Frankie. It was hard to tell because of the square-shouldered costume, but he must be in high school, too. If he was a regular member of the Butler Brats, the informal nickname of the youth theater group, then wouldn't Kaia know him? She was treating him with cool distance, the way she always treated someone she hadn't made up her mind about yet.

"So you don't know what happened?" I asked again as we stepped aside for a stream of people leaving the theater. They were nervous, murmuring in muted concern.

He turned to me, his forehead creased. "I have to go," he said, and brushed past me to push against the flow of the crowd.

"Why didn't he want to tell us?" I asked.

Kaia put her hands in her pockets. "Maybe we don't inspire confidence."

"And you don't know who he is?"

She shrugged. "Frankie."

It seemed to take forever to push our way back up to the balcony. It was deserted. We found my tote and sketchbook and Kaia's purse stuffed beneath our seats. "Fabulous," I muttered, drawing my cell phone from its pocket in my tote. "Where do you think Livvie went?"

Kaia scanned the rows. "She couldn't have gotten far."

I pecked out a text and sent it:

Where are you?

The reply was swift:

Mom just picked me up.

"Oh, no," I said and handed the phone to Kaia. If Livvie's mom called my mom before I did, there would be chaos.

Kaia's eyes widened and she handed the phone back. She pulled her own phone from her pocket and texted her mom. "We need to get out of here. Before Dad shows up with the police."

"Too late, the police are already here." I pulled her to the edge of the balcony. Two uniformed officers were walking up the center aisle to where a small group gathered around a middle-aged couple. It was the pair that was behind us in line while we waited for the doors to open! The lady who'd smiled at Livvie's dramatics was perched on a stretcher, but she was talking to the officer standing nearest to her. I could hear her wavering voice but couldn't make out the words. "Let's go downstairs."

Kaia plucked my phone from my fingers. "I'm telling your mom you're fine and that we're heading home."

"We are … in five minutes."

I crept down the stairs and looped around to the side door of the theater's main floor, down the farthest aisle, trying not to draw attention to myself. The police were tuned in to the victim, and a few patrons were straggled toward the doors. One young couple was still seated in the middle rows, enraptured with one another, seemingly oblivious to the confusion around them. They had come to sit in the theater together, and that's what they were going to do.

I was close enough now to hear the man's deep voice, angry and shaken. "...and that's when he grabbed her purse," he said. "She tried to hold on to it, so he hit her." The man's voice shook. "He just hit her–bam!–like that." The man made a fist and swung it toward the officer's jaw. "What kind of a person would hit a woman like that?" he asked, turning to his wife as an EMT leaned closer to shine a light in her eyes. Guess someone would need an ambulance tonight, after all.

"Looking for something?" Frankie stepped in front of me, blocking my view.

"Is she okay? We were next to them in line," I said, refocusing on him. He had taken off the boxy-shouldered coat, and his sandy hair was flattened and sticking up in odd places from the mask. "I mean, why would someone take her purse?" I gestured to the rows of empty seats. "Why her, out of all these people?"

He frowned. "I think it's time for you to leave. The show's over."

*　　　　*　　　　*　　　　*　　　　*

Livvie popped a green grape into her mouth. "So he just told you to get out?"

"Pretty much." I watched Kyle McFadden cross the cafeteria, his plate piled high with only a pyramid of garlic bread, no spaghetti. I'd have to steer clear of him in fifth period, when we usually shared a work table in study hall. Garlic breath.

"Ursula, I'm really sorry if your parents were mad. When you guys left me sitting up there," she cast a mournful look at me, "I just sort of freaked out."

14

"I'm the sorry one. I wasn't thinking about leaving you. I just saw that Frankenstein running and, I don't know." I shook my head. "It looked so wrong. And I didn't think; I chased."

"So what'd your parents say?"

"They were cool about it. Kaia's, too. In fact, Frankie was the only one who seemed tense." I scooted a grain of rice around the bottom of my lunch container.

"Forget him," Livvie said, picking up another grape. "Unless he was really cute. Like, seriously cute."

I frowned.

"He was?! *Seriously* cute?"

I shrugged. "I can't stop thinking about that poor woman and her husband. Why would someone pick her? I mean, they were dressed in nice clothes, but I wouldn't say they looked, you know, rich. What got his attention, do you think?"

Livvie shuddered. "I can't stop thinking about her screaming— so scary. I thought it was part of the show."

"It doesn't make sense for a person to go through the trouble of dressing up like a monster just to steal a random purse. That parking lot is super dark. It would be way easier to wait there and mug someone."

"You worry me sometimes," Livvie said, twisting her empty baggie into a wad. "Did you at least get any good drawings for the newsletter?"

I sighed. "Not really. Alex will not be happy."

Livvie rolled her eyes. "When is Alex *ever* happy?"

*   *   *   *   *

"My art director didn't bring me any art?" The editor of the East River Christian School blog, *The Roar,* leaned against the desk and crossed his freckled arms.

"I'm the blog's art director, not yours," I said. I already felt myself bristling, and took a deep breath. I didn't want to fight with him, but Alex could get under my skin so fast.

He gave me a crushing glare. "I can fire you, you know. "

Sarcasm bubbled up. "For getting evacuated out of a theater? Right. Who else in the school is crazy enough to do this job?" Or desperate. I needed this. I needed deadlines, work, experience. More than anything, I wanted to get accepted to art college. But not just any art college—Northwestern. To do that, I needed to push myself. And to push myself, I needed Alex's help. He was in charge of the blog, the school newsletter, and the website. "Besides, Lowe would have to approve the firing, and you know he'd never do that."

"What firing?"

I spun in my chair. Principal Lowe, blowing on the surface of his coffee, walked to the desk where Alex was sitting. He took a sip, and the steam fogged his glasses.

I tried to keep the whine from my voice. "Alex is going to fire me because I didn't get any sketches from the Butler last night."

"Hmm. Saw the story on the news this morning. You were there?"

I nodded. "With Livvie and Kaia."

"Ursula's right," said Lowe. "You can't fire her for that."

I shot Alex a smug grin.

"But, you can fire her for insubordination," he said.

"I'm considering it," said Alex, tapping his fingers on the desk.

"Mister Lowe!"

"But, before he fires you, Ursula, I'd quit." Lowe pulled a chair up to the desk and set his coffee mug on a sticky note. "You have too much talent to let a tyrant like him push you around."

"Wait, whose side are you on?" I asked.

He smiled. "I never take sides. How was the movie? Until the hullabaloo?"

I told him everything that happened. "I did get these two quick ones," I said, turning my sketchbook to the ceiling sketch. I let them see that page before I flipped to the outline of Frankie and the audience. "Here's Frankenstein."

"Frankenstein is the scientist; that's Frankenstein's monster," Alex said in that know-it-all tone. It was pretty much his only tone.

"Very nice," Lowe murmured, adjusting the sleek frames of his glasses then scooting the corner of the sketchbook carefully with his index finger. "I think your editor should use this with your movie review."

"What review? I only saw the first twenty minutes."

He pointed his index finger in the air and my heart sank. I knew he'd gotten an idea, one that probably meant more work for me. "You can review it from an ERCS teen's perspective. Discuss how the plot approaches faith in God. Great idea! You can rent it, right?"

"Stream it," Alex corrected, turning to the computer. He was always editing people, even the teachers. He put his fingers to the keyboard and began typing.

"I think that's my cue," Lowe said, and stood. "Crisis averted." He paused at the doorway. "I'm sure the library has the movie, too."

17

Chapter Three

The smell of the Jewel Valley Public Library intoxicates me. No matter how busy I am on a research paper, how hyped-up on the adrenaline of procrastination, the smell of the library instantly soothes my nerves. When I push through the door and into the foyer, I always take a deep breath and hold it in my lungs for a few seconds. I swear, it's aromatherapy. Probably because the smell is paper and ink, two of my earliest obsessions. When I was little, I tried to eat paper. Mom had to watch and yank it out of my mouth or I'd devour it. Truthfully, I still feel like I could live on paper and ink, somehow. And hot chocolate.

I walked into the library and felt a rush of expectation. Think of the things a person could learn, all neatly shelved in alphabetical order. Kaia would say the internet is like that, too, but books are different. They're mysterious, and they take time— especially for me. Reading is still hard work, and that makes books more personal. In a way, they're sort of my frenemies. I always feel like going through the stacks and running my fingertips along their spines. But that's another weird thing about me.

I headed for the New Arrivals section. It didn't take me long to spot a book on drawing graphic novels. I slid it into my tote, then went to the DVD section. I circled the table, but there was a guy blocking the 'F's. Great. I pretended to peruse the 'S' section. When he turned around, I couldn't keep the astonishment from showing on my face. It was Frankie.

He seemed as surprised as I was.

I laughed. "What are you—no, wait, let me guess. Frankenstein?" I pointed at the DVD in his hand. "Research?"

His expression chilled. "There's another copy."

"I'm sorry. I didn't mean to be nosy."

"I have to go," he said, and passed me. I grabbed the other disc and followed him to the checkout counter.

"Have you heard anything about the woman from the theater?" I asked, then kicked myself. If I was trying to convince him that I wasn't nosy, it wasn't a good follow-up question.

He turned his head slightly, but didn't look at me. "Why would I hear about her?"

"Well," I said, trying to keep my voice light and conversational, "you work at the theater. I mean, don't you?"

He didn't answer.

"But my friend, Kaia, didn't recognize you. Do you know her? She's in the Butler Brats."

"No."

I could tell he was conflicted. He didn't want to talk to me, but he seemed to want to know something about the youth group. If I was going to find out anything, I had to keep him interested. "You must be new."

"Not that new," he retorted.

I paused to give him time to meet me half-way, but he didn't take the bait. Time to bluff. "I guess you're probably too old to be in the Brats. When do you graduate?"

He frowned. "Next year."

"Oh, then you're good."

He stepped to the counter and slid the DVD to the librarian. Her name was Debbie, and I adored her. "Your library card?" she asked.

He tried to speak so I wouldn't hear, and I had mercy on him and turned away, fiddling with my phone. "I need to get a card. I just moved."

"Are you eighteen?"

"No."

"I'm so sorry, but you have to have a parent or guardian come in to apply for one." She looked sympathetic, then tactfully swung her gaze toward me. "Hey, Ursula, how are you? All set?"

"Yes, thank you." I slid the disc and my library card across the counter and glanced at Frankie. "Do you want to borrow it from me?" I asked.

He looked toward the exit. Debbie wordlessly ran the bar code scanner over my card and handed it back to me. "No," he said. "Thanks."

I took the due date slip, the disc, and the book and slid them into my tote. "We can watch it in the media lab at my school. There's basketball practice tonight, so someone will be around to unlock it for me."

He seemed torn. "No. That's okay." He started for the door.

I followed and caught up to him on the sidewalk. "At least give me your number so I can loan it to you."

He sighed. "Fine." He waited for me to fish my phone free, then mumbled the number as I keyed it into my contacts.

"Are you sure you don't want to watch it tonight?" I gave him my most non-threatening smile. It was as bold as I'd ever been, basically asking a guy to a movie. I guess curiosity made me brave.

He looked up and down the street and frowned, then stuffed his hands in his pockets. "I'm sure. See you around." He strode to the corner and disappeared behind the building.

*   *   *   *   *

"He said he would see you around," Livvie said, leaning her shoulder into my arm and swirling her fries in a puddle of ketchup. "That's good, right?"

"I don't know." I chewed my lip and pushed a straw paper into a droplet of moisture on my water glass. "I'm not sure yet."

She rolled her eyes and made an appealing gesture at Kaia. "Tell her that's a good thing."

Kaia pushed her plate toward the edge of the table and craned her neck to look for a waitress. "She's smart to be cautious," she said. "You weren't with us at the Butler, in the alley. He was … rude."

"Rude and cute," Livvie muttered.

"I asked around," said Kaia. "He did come in the summer, just like you thought."

"How did you know?" Livvie asked me.

"Well, if he was a real theater nerd, like Kaia——no offense——"

"None taken." She took a sip of her root beer float.

"——then he'd be in the Butler Brats, right? So I knew, or guessed, that maybe he moved here in the summer." I turned to Kaia. "Did you know the other Frankensteins?"

She shook her head. "Only one. Derek. He's the one who got chewing gum stuck in his nose when we were in primary grades, remember?"

Grade levels were all relevant for Kaia. She was homeschooled, and her years were a little more fluid than mine or Livvie's. She could have graduated this year if she wanted. Instead, she decided to take two college classes, along with

21

calculus and a foreign language. I was taking Spanish I, but Kaia had selected Japanese. "Why Japanese?" I'd wondered.

Kaia shrugged. "Why not? It's a fascinating culture."

"But if you took Spanish, we could speak it around other people to keep our conversations private."

Kaia had given me a look of surprise. "Spanish is hardly secret. If you want to have a private language, we'd almost have to make up our own."

We'd spent two afternoons crafting the beginnings of a language we named Schnonk, but then we got bored and gave it up.

"Gum in the nose." Livvie shook her head ruefully. "That's a tough one to live down. It really sticks to you, know what I mean?"

I groaned. "Awful."

"That was actually pretty good," Kaia said.

"Thanks. So who were the other two Frankensteins?"

She shook her head. "There was another guy, the son of one of the ushers. But the fourth Frankenstein ... " She smoothed the cuff of her sweater. "No one knows. There should have only been three Franks. They were supposed to keep the audience interested during the movie. They wanted it to be memorable."

"It was memorable, for sure." Livvie shivered

"Especially for the woman who was robbed." I pushed away what was left of the fries I was sharing with Liv.

She dropped her head in her hands. "I have to meet this guy and see for myself if you're making a huge mistake. I don't get why we're worrying about a lady's purse and ignoring the obvious: the new guy who needs friends." She wagged her eyebrows and looked so funny, I couldn't help laughing. Kaia smiled and shook her head.

"It's time to go," I said, grabbing my tote and pushing Liv out of the vinyl booth. "Are you coming with us?"

Kaia shook her head and held up her phone. "Dad's picking me up on his way home from the grocery. Then I get to drive the rest of the way."

Kaia had her permit already but no car. Livvie'd flunked her test three times, and I was studying extra hard. I didn't really need a permit yet since I loved to ride my bike everywhere in town. But I also sort of dreaded taking the test. I knew I could tell them I had dyslexia and take the audio test, but I wanted to pass the regular test on my first try. And I was procrastinating. But Kaia had so many siblings she had to get her license right away to help drive them. I felt sorry for her poor dad, doing the grocery shopping for seven people. No wonder he wanted to pick her up to help. "Okay. Text me when you get home."

"I will." She waved as Livvie and I left.

I noticed how the trees looked a little more bare, even since yesterday. And the days were shorter. After daylight savings ended in a couple of weeks, it would be hard to make it home from school before the sun set. I'd have to put the headlight and taillight on my bike. I didn't mind because I'd found some adorable disco-style lights on vacation this year and couldn't wait to use them. I loved to decorate my bike.

A thought struck me. Would a purse thief be interested in cool bikes? The possibility made me feel cold all over. Hopefully the police would find him soon.

"I hate how everything is dying," Livvie said, wrinkling her nose. "And I hate that winter is coming, too."

"But that's when all the magic happens, isn't it?" I kicked at an acorn.

"What are you talking about? What magic?" She tugged her sweater tighter around her.

I shrugged. "Think of some magic. I bet it happened in the

cold or the dark. I think that's when miracles happen."

She thought. When she spoke, she sounded glum. "I can't think of any magic."

"What? Yes, you can."

"Well, what magic are you talking about?"

"Mmm … Okay, how about Christmas?"

"Kaia's always telling people Christmas is fake, Jesus was born in the Spring."

"No, she doesn't think it's fake, but that's *why* we celebrate it in December. Don't we need a little magic and mystery and sparkly lights? A light in the darkest time of year?"

She shrugged and rubbed her arms. "Yeah, I guess so. I still hate the cold, though. I just want to wear my flip flops all year. Flip-flop weather. That's all I need."

"Maybe you'll move some place you can wear them all year."

Livvie stopped and grew serious. "Don't ever move away, okay?"

I turned to look at her. "I said *you* could move, not me."

"I'm not moving, and I don't want you too, either. Promise."

I took her hand and rubbed it between both of mine to warm it up. "You know I want to get in to Northwestern." *Will get in*, I added to myself. It was all I'd wanted since Mom and I visited last year after researching art programs online. "Besides, that's probably not something either of us should promise. It's like Mrs. Sims says, 'We don't know where God is going to take us.'" It was one of our geography teacher's favorite sayings. When she said it, my heart always beat a little faster. I hoped He took me someplace exciting.

Her eyes glittered in the light of the street lamp. "He's not going to take us away from one another. I don't think I could handle it."

My stomach felt like it dropped into my shoes. I tried to smile and tugged her until she began walking again. "Stop worrying about something that hasn't happened yet."

"Hey, can I stay at your house tonight?" she asked abruptly.

"Why—is anything wrong?"

She pouted. "If you don't want me to, that's fine."

"You know I do. Talk to me, Liv. What's going on?"

"Nothing," she said. "It's not a big deal."

"I was going to watch Frankenstein tonight so I can loan it to Frankie tomorrow." The thought of the DVD in my tote nagged at me ever since I'd left the library. I was dying to see it, in grainy black and white, to put pencil to pure white paper and use the pause button to get the sketches I wanted. "Alex is on my back to make graphics for the blog, and now Lowe wants me to review the movie. Why don't you come over and watch it with me? You can help me with the review; you know I'm terrible at writing. We'll make a tent in my room like we used to."

The corner of her mouth trembled, almost melting to a smile, but she shook her head. "No way. I wouldn't be able to sleep at all after watching that."

We stopped in front of my house. She cast one short glance at it before waving. Her breath came out in plumes. "See you tomorrow." She walked toward her own house, one block up and across Bluebird Street. We would always watch for the safe signal. While I waited, I studied my house, too. If God took me someplace exciting, I'd have to leave all this in about a year and a half! The thought made me feel a little sad, at least until visions of cities, art scenes, and new places swept it away.

When Livvie's porch light blinked twice, I ducked into the house and flicked my switch twice, too. Mom was on the sofa, flipping through a gardening magazine with the tv on mute. I don't know how she can read and watch tv at the same time, but she does. "How are the Other Two?" she asked.

I draped my scarf and jacket on a hook by the door. That's what she called my friends. The Other Two. "They're good. Well, Kaia's good."

Mom closed the magazine. "What's wrong with Livvie Lou?"

"I'm not sure, actually." I flopped onto the striped armchair and pulled my tote onto my lap. "She asked to stay over, but I told her I was going to finish watching Frankenstein and that she might not want to stay tonight." I raised my eyes, heavy with guilt. "I didn't mean to make it sound like she wasn't welcome, or that I didn't want her. But she got kind of ... offended, I think."

"That doesn't sound like her," Mom said, uncurling her legs and sliding her slender feet into worn moccasins.

"I know. But I'm not sure she was really offended. I think it may have been a cover up. I asked if anything happened. She said no. I'm a little confused and worried."

Mom clicked her tongue in her mouth in that way she did, and gave me a look of sympathy. "I'm sure she's hurting. But maybe you should give her a little space. Let her know you're there for her, but let her come to you about it when she's ready."

"It's just so hard. Before the divorce, we felt closer."

"I know, Little Bear. Keep praying for her. This is going to be a big adjustment."

She hadn't called me Little Bear for a while, and I felt like a kid again, cherished and safe. When they were in college, Dad asked Mom to marry him while they were stargazing, during the Leonid meteor shower. That's how I was almost named Leona. But they saved the name for my brother, Leo, and I got Ursula, instead. Ursula meant 'bear'. Dad liked to joke that he had a zoo— a bear and a lion.

Ugh, my name. Sometimes Dad calls me Ursa Major, especially when I get a good grade or something. He's full of cringey nicknames. But truth is, I kind of like them.

I smiled. "I am praying."

"Me, too. She's lucky to have friends like you and Kaia." She stood and squeezed my shoulder on her way to the kitchen. "Some hot chocolate?"

I puffed out my cheeks. "No, thanks. I'm still stuffed from Wenzinger's. Besides, I want to get started on this." I pulled the DVD from my tote and showed her. "Alex wants some illustrations, like, yesterday."

She clucked again. "Slave driver."

"Tell me about it."

"Homework?"

"Just the drawings."

"Don't forget to do your laundry. And don't stay up too late."

I yawned, then laughed. "I don't think I could. 'Night."

"Goodnight." She blew me a kiss, then popped a marshmallow into her mug.

Chapter Four

Once in my room, I clicked on the lamp and opened the DVD player on my old, reliable desktop computer. I named her Buzzy, mostly because of the sounds she made when I fired her up. I nestled the disc into its place and started the player. Skipping through the scene selection until I found the right one—after the monster came to life—I settled onto my bed. That was when the Frankensteins had been loosed at the Butler, when Livvie had nearly come unglued.

Now, alone and in my own bedroom, the movie seemed creepier than it had in the festive balcony of the Butler. "God?" Frankenstein yelled. "Now I know what it feels like to be God!"

Whoa, Principal Lowe would love that line for the review. I hit pause and made some notes, then laid out a quick sketch. Steadying my hand, I tried not to shudder as I drew the crazy scientist, with his lab smock flapping wildly, his eyes turned to heaven. It seemed like it was the same big mistake over and over again with people. We think we can be equal to God, that we can outsmart Him, somehow.

A few weeks ago, my science class had been caught up in a loud, hot discussion about cloning, first extinct species, and then, of course, humans. The class was divided between those who thought creating human clones was unethical and immoral, and those who argued that the research could be used to treat tragic medical problems. At the time, I wasn't sure how I felt about it. Both sides had made good points. Now, though, I thought I could see the danger in trying to play God. Or ignoring Him. It's like the movie was about more than just the story of a guy and his science project. I jotted down a few more notes.

I hit the play button and put the finishing touches on the drawing, listening to the movie, and glancing up at the screen every once in a while. But when Frankenstein's friends tried to reason with him, the arrogance of his answer paralyzed my drawing hand, raising goosebumps. I was glued to the screen. "Poor old Waldman," Frankenstein said. "Have you never wanted to do something that was dangerous?"

I hit pause again. The impostor at the theater had wanted to do something dangerous. But why? If Dr. Frankenstein was blinded by his obsession, and by his pride, then the thief had an obsession, too. I just had to find out what it was. And if, like the doctor, he was too proud, maybe it was possible for me to discover the motive.

Pride. Everyone had it, and we had to fight to control it. I studied the Henry Frankenstein's face on the screen, luminous in black-and-white. What happens when we stop trying to control it, and give in to it? I shivered, remembering the lady's scream from the Butler. Bad things. Very bad things.

* * * * *

Can you come to Wenzinger's after school?
For the movie?

29

I'll be there.

I showed the texts to Livvie while we huddled in the lunchroom before school started.

"Hook, line, and sinker," she said, handing the phone back to me. "Nicely done."

"I'm not actually trying to catch him," I said.

"But you *are* fishing for something," she said, snapping her gum. "Aren't you? What do you want to find?"

I shifted my tote higher onto my shoulder. It was heavy. Today I'd brought my sketchbook as always, but also my special inking pens and markers so I could finish my artwork before I submitted it to Alex after lunch. "I'm not sure exactly. But I think he knows something." It was the first time I'd admitted it out loud. It was something about the way he'd pulled his mask off at the Butler when he heard there was another Frankenstein. And the way he'd been so gruff with Kaia and me that night.

"Ugh, I wish you'd drop it about the purse."

"I was hoping you could come."

She barked a dry laugh. "I don't want to be the third wheel. Especially if you're going to interrogate a cute guy. Awkward."

That hurt a little. "I wasn't going to interrogate him, I just—"

"None of this matters, anyway," she said, grabbing her books and clutching them to her chest. "I'm going to class."

I watched her leave the lunchroom, the door swinging shut behind her. What was *that* about? When Livvie got upset, she needed time to cool off. Any attempt to talk through it would be met with a sullen silence.

The bell rang. Hopefully, she'd be ready to talk by third period.

I joined the stampede and moved through the hall.

        *   *   *   *   *

Alex chewed the end of his pen thoughtfully. "Livvie is mad at you."

"This, I know," I muttered, arranging my sketch on the scanner. It was actually a copy machine that could scan, and we only had permission to use it for the two class periods right after lunch. During the first week of school, the secretary gave us a three-day-long tutorial on how to operate it. She made some subtle threats about what might happen to a student who broke the copy machine, and reluctantly left us to do our work.

"*Why* is she mad at you?"

"This, I don't know."

Alex glanced at me. "You must have an idea"

I sighed and crossed the office to sit at the computer. "It's kind of a long story. And I'm probably wrong about why she's upset. In fact, I'm probably wrong about all of it." I clicked the mouse with enough force to emphasize my point.

He switched the pen to the other side of his mouth and spoke around it. "Doubting yourself."

For a moment, the hum of the copy machine was the only sound. I turned to him. "Like I'm going to talk to the school's only reporter about any of this."

He put his hands up in defense. "Like I'm going to make the only other member of the school blog mad at me."

I turned back to the screen. "I'm meeting Frankenstein after school to loan him a movie."

If he was confused, he didn't let it show. "Doctor Frankenstein or his monster? Which movie?"

"Frankenstein."

31

"Of course, of course."

I shot him a look. "I don't know his real name yet."

"So, not the one that stole the purse, right?"

"No. The other one."

"Ah."

I swiveled the chair around to face him. "Yeah, about the purse."

"What about the purse?" He was repeating what I said in the form of a question to draw out my story. I'd watched him do it to other people several times, but I didn't care. No one else had been this interested in my obsession, except for Kaia.

"Exactly, right? Why take that purse? Why the disguise? Why grab it in front of an entire theater of people? That's risky. So it had to be for a reason." I blinked. Wow, Alex's method really worked. Hearing my ideas aloud made me realize they were true. "It had to be *that* lady, *that* night."

He leaned on the corner of the desk, his uniform maroon polo shirt untucked and wrinkled. "All good questions, ones that an investigative reporter would ask."

"But I'm not an investigative reporter," I said, making a formatting change to the sketch on the computer. "I'm an artist. Besides, I saw your face when I gave you the notes for my movie review. Obviously writing isn't my strong point."

He shrugged. "True, but I'm giving you a temporary promotion. Go find answers."

"Oh, no." I stared at him. Horror gripped my heart.

"What?"

I pointed. "Is that *my* pen?" He twirled one of my Pentel Energels in his fingers. The end of the cap had molar marks and shone faintly with drool.

He held up the pen. "Oops."

I watched the door for fifteen minutes. Each time it opened, I tensed, then relaxed when it turned out to be someone else. By the time Frankie finally ducked into the restaurant, out of the chilly wind, I had nearly given up. He scanned the dining room and nodded when he saw me. Unzipping his hoodie, he sat on the edge of the booth, avoiding eye contact.

"Hi," I said, too brightly, and kicked myself. "My friends and I have been calling you Frankie. I'm sorry I never asked your real name."

I had managed not to ask for it outright, and for a moment, I was sure he wasn't going to tell me. "It's Frank," he said.

"Are you serious?"

"No."

"Oh." I clutched my tote on my lap. He was not getting that blessed movie until he at least told me a real name. I glanced at the soda counter. I could yelp if he tried to snatch the disc from me. Oh, my word, the night at the Butler had made me paranoid.

"It's Matt."

"Matthew?"

He blinked, but kept his voice even. "Matthias. Just Matt."

I slid the DVD across the dappled plastic tabletop. "Have you seen this before? I mean, before the other night?"

He took the plastic sleeve and turned it over to scan the back cover. "No. You?"

"Huh-uhn. It was … Well, I'll let you watch it and decide for yourself, I guess. So, how long have you been into acting? I thought you were just dressing up at the Butler because of the Frankenstein factor. But, since you haven't seen the movie, I guess that rules you out as a fan, right?"

I watched him open his backpack and tuck the disc gently between the pages of a textbook. "Kind of a long story."

"I've got an hour or so," I shot back. "It can't take *that* long, can it?" I sipped my hot chocolate. I could tell he was weighing how much to say to me, trying to gauge if I was trustworthy. I didn't blame him. It would be strange to be in a new town, to try and determine who might be a friend.

"My uncle's on the theater's board of directors."

I nodded, then pointed at the textbook. "Do you go to Arthur?"

Arthur High School was a large, squat, yellow brick complex at the heart of town. I'd been there for a few events over the years. In fact, last spring Kaia, Livvie and I had seen a multi-instrumentalist from Ecuador perform at the A.H.S. auditorium. The school was so much bigger than East River. Kaia, home-schooled nearly from birth, explored the halls. "East River doesn't smell like this," I said, sniffing with interest.

"Our school smells like french fries and eraser shavings," Livvie echoed. "I think Arthur smells like a castle."

We had collapsed into a fit of giggling, and I smiled now at the thought. Did Matt think Arthur smelled like a castle?

He only nodded.

"How do you like it?"

He shrugged. "How do *you* like it?"

"I don't go there."

Finally, I said something that grabbed his attention. He frowned. "I thought it was the only high school in town."

"Only public school."

"You go to private school?" His wall of suspicion was back up.

"East River Christian. Almost one hundred in the upper grades, and about that many in the lower grades, too. You didn't wonder why I was wearing the same outfit both times you've seen me after school?" I plucked my maroon polo shirt from my shoulder and wagged the sleeve at him.

He digested this. "I didn't notice."

"Subject change." I leaned forward. "Does it make any sense to you that the lady from the other night would get robbed during the show?"

If he was suspicious before, he was on lock-down now. The dim light of curiosity in his eyes extinguished. I back-pedaled. "Sorry. I can tell you don't want to talk about it." I sighed and smiled, trying to put him back at ease. "I can talk about other things, I promise. It's just been hard for me to shake the sound of that lady screaming. She was behind us in line before the movie started, and seemed so nice."

"I have to go," he said, knocking his knee hard against the booth as he slid out of the seat.

"Oof! You okay?"

"Fine," he said, slinging his backpack over his shoulder. "Thanks for the movie." He strode to the door and left.

*   *   *   *   *

On Fridays, Kaia biked to East River for lunch. She looked from Livvie to me, her dark brows raised. "So ... ?"

I glanced at Livvie. She had, apparently, not filled Kaia in about why she was mad at me. Her body language was set to deep freeze. Okay, elephant in the room. No big deal.

"Yeah, tell us about your date, Urs," she said without enthusiasm.

"Yeah, Urs," Alex echoed, sliding his tray next to Kaia and taking the empty seat. Kaia had become a fixture at the East River

35

cafeteria on Fridays, and all the students knew her. "Do tell."

Livvie furiously smashed her baked potato open.

I crossed my arms and gripped my elbows to keep from shaking Livvie. "He came. I gave him the movie. Then he left."

"No information?" he asked.

"His name is Matt, not Frankie. That pretty much sums it up." I sighed. "Told you I'm not an investigative journalist."

He answered around a mouthful of baked chicken. "You just need to practice. Stick with me, kid, I'll teach you everything I know."

I bristled a little. He was a year older than me and often talked to us like he was our grandpa, or some sort of nerdy, red-haired guru.

"That should take at least an hour," Livvie muttered, and Alex rewarded her with a sarcastic grin. I smirked. She was beginning to thaw.

Kaia watched Blake Kupfner cross the cafeteria, heading for the gym. I was sure she had a big, fat crush on the tall basketball player, but knew better than to press her about it. As the door swung closed behind Blake, Kaia said, "He has an older brother."

I blinked. "Who does?"

"Frankie. Matt."

"Seemingly irrelevant," Alex said, stabbing his plastic fork at me, "but you never know. File that away."

"Where?"

He tapped his temple with an index finger. "In your brain. A good journalist keeps this stuff in her mind."

"I have too much in there already. Besides, my brain works in weird ways."

"Well, scoot the sea horses and robots over and make some room for the answers," he said, polishing off the rest of his lunch and tossing a crumpled napkin onto the tray.

I scowled. "Stay out of my folders." I had files on the school computer where I stored my doodles.

"What?" he asked, standing to leave. "I was looking for clip art for the Humane Society story. Later, Kaia."

"See you," she said, amused. She waited until he walked away and smiled at Livvie. "He's … unique."

Livvie gave her mangled potato one final poke. "That's a nice way to put it." She finally faced me. "Are you going to leave this robbery stuff alone now, or have you recruited Alex to teach you how to creep around looking for stories that don't exist?"

I tried to swallow the frustration, and took a deep breath before responding. "I'm not creeping around, but I'm not going to stop asking questions, either," I said carefully.

She scoffed and held out a hand to Kaia. "Tell her to drop it. The police were there, what more can she do?"

Kaia tilted her head, her eyes crinkling at the edges. "I know you're worried."

At that, Livvie deflated. The cafeteria was half-empty now, and the bell was going to ring in a few minutes. When she spoke, her voice was very small. "Nothing good can come of this. Not even a cute guy."

Kaia patted her on the arm. "We're not going to be heroes, here. We're just going to do a little…exploring."

My heart lifted. We? Kaia was in.

"You guys always talk me into doing crazy stuff."

"Think of how much excitement it brings to your life. You know you love it," Kaia said.

"I don't love it," she murmured. "I love peace."

Kaia and I exchanged a look. 'Peace' and 'Livvie' were not two words that fit together.

"I think it's time we went back to the Butler," said Kaia, but the bell rang before she could finish her thought. Break was over.

37

Chapter 5

"It was just terrible, poor thing!" The lady bobbed her head, her hairsprayed butterscotch-colored curls frozen in place. "She was treated and released, that's what I heard. Shook up more than anything, really."

"Did you see anyone out of the ordinary that night?" Kaia asked her. A group of girls our age pushed through the lobby doors and went into the auditorium.

"Bless your heart!" Mrs. Betty Kreps, longtime ticket booth volunteer at the Butler, touched her fingertips to her throat. "You sound just like the police. No! All was perfectly quiet as usual in the lobby. Once in a while, someone came out to stretch their legs, or to run a little one to the restroom. That always happens. But the ticket booth was calm. I had all my money counted and the deposit filled out." She paled. "What if that punk had come out to the lobby and robbed *me*? It's a good thing most criminals are short on smarts! I don't know how much money that poor dear in there had in her purse, but if he had used his head, and looked around—why! We had a nearly full-house that night." She shook her head. "He could have gotten away with much more. Not that I'm trying to coach thieves, you two."

"No," Kaia said. "You wouldn't happen to know the victim's

name, would you? Have they released it?"

"They have not," said Mrs. Kreps firmly, shaking her stiff hair. I couldn't help thinking it looked like cotton candy. She lowered her voice and watched another couple enter the theater. "But one of my friends at church is her cousin."

I held my breath. How could we ask for her name?

"Does she think the police are going to catch the thief?" Kaia asked.

Mrs. Kreps frowned. "We all worry it's not very high on their priorities. The drugs! Who can believe the drugs, in a town like this? And times are tough, all over. They just don't have as many officers as they need. No, a stolen purse isn't likely to be much of a concern. Besides, the purse itself was already found."

My heart skipped. "What? It was?"

She nodded. "Just a few blocks from here. All that was missing was the cash. My friend said he left all her cards. So, no harm done, I suppose. I mean, to the purse, obviously. There was harm to her." She tsk-tsked. "All the same, makes me nervous to be in the ticket booth alone now. What if he comes back?"

"I think you'll be safe. Maybe Richard can sit with you," Kaia said.

Mrs. Kreps smiled. "Such a nice man. You'd never know it from the look of him. So burly, and that beard! It looks like he sleeps in the dirty clothes hamper half the time. But a real sweetheart."

"I work for my school newsblog. Can you ask your friend if I could interview her cousin? I'd be very professional." I tried to sound professional, and hoped I nailed it.

The older woman seemed amused. "I'll ask, honey. Let me have your phone number, and I'll let you know. I'll give you a call tomorrow."

She handed me a slip of paper and I wrote my number on it.

She took it with raised brows. "What's a newsblog?" she asked.

*   *   *   *   *

Livvie rang the doorbell promptly at nine. Every week, my family had our Spark Saturday Pancake Breakfast. Friends were welcome, and Livvie usually came down the street to join us. I swung the door wide for her to come in. "Oh, my gosh, I hate cold weather," she said, leaping into the living room and stamping her slippered feet. She shed her parka. She'd put on a sweater but was still in her pajama bottoms. So was I, and Leo was in his full Spider-Man pajama glory.

"And it's only October! Come on in," Mom called from the kitchen. She grabbed another plate from the cupboard and set Livvie's place at the table.

"What'll it be, Livvie Lou?" Dad boomed from his station at the stove. "Chocolate chips or plain? That's what's on today's menu."

"Plain, please," she said, sliding into the chair. She gratefully accepted the cup of hot chocolate Mom put in front of her, and cupped her hands around the warm ceramic mug.

Leo pushed up his glasses and burped. His upper lip had sprouted a hot chocolate mustache.

"Leo," Mom said.

"'Scuse me," he muttered, casting a glance at Dad. "It's just Liv."

"Thanks," Livvie said, and blew on the surface of her drink.

"What's new with you, Lou?" Dad asked, reaching for her plate. He'd started calling her Livvie Lou almost from the start, and now Mom did, too. Liv didn't seem to mind, but sometimes it made me cringe.

She handed the plate to him. "Nothing."

He sighed melodramatically. "You always say that."

She winced. "Uhm. I'm singing a solo in the Christmas play at school."

"Great!" said Mom.

I put down my fork. "I didn't know that."

"I just found out on Wednesday."

"Better not mess up," Leo said, hacking his sausage link into bits with his butter knife. "There's always a thousand people there."

"I don't think there are *that* many," Mom said, then turned to Livvie. "You'll do great."

"And what about this Frankenstein caper?" asked Dad, returning her plate with a large pancake. He stalked, stiff-legged, to his place at the table, making a horrible monster face.

"Ugh," she said, shuddering. "I should never have let Urs and Kaia talk me into going to the movie." She shot me a look, and muttered, "I'm *always* letting them talk me into things."

I sipped my orange juice.

"Watch out! I think I saw something in the shadows of Bluebird Street ... " Dad raised his eyebrows and stuffed a forkful of pancakes into his mouth.

"Don't do that to me, Timbo! You'll make me have nightmares."

He cackled an evil laugh.

"How are your parents doing, honey?" Mom asked. She was the only one who could get away with questions like that.

A moment passed, but Livvie didn't let it last too long. "They're...okay. It's just been really weird. I'll have two Thanksgivings, two Christmases, you know? It's going to be so different."

"It must be," Mom said, patting Livvie's hand. "We'll be doing our same-old, same-old, if you need a break."

"Thanks," she said. "I think they both have sort of lost their minds right now. Hopefully…" She trailed off.

Leo scooted his chair away from the table and it made a honking sound on the tile floor. "I'm going to play Rocket League," he said.

"Uh." Mom got his attention and wagged a finger at his dishes. He grunted and carried them to the sink, then ran to the living room and threw himself onto the couch.

"I, for one, will be performing my annual Thanksgiving concert here at the Spark Residence," offered Dad, and he sang the first line of his made-up Thanksgiving song, "Away in the Mayflower", in a screeching, off-key howl. All of his Thanksgiving songs were revamped Christmas carols, but he changed the lyrics.

Livvie and I grimaced. "Dad," I begged, trying hard to keep the whine out of my voice.

But Mom blew him a kiss. "Bravo!" she said.

"Uh, thanks. But I might have to be busy that night," said Livvie.

*   *   *   *   *

Later that day, my cell rang with a number I didn't recognize. "Hello?"

"Yes, hello, this is Betty Kreps?"

"Oh, hi." I swung my legs off the bed and scrabbled on my desk for my notepad and a marker. "How are you?"

"Fine, dear. I saw my friend at choir this morning and she called her cousin, Susanne, right up."

My heart leaped at the mention of her name—Susanne! "She did?"

"Yes, and when she heard you were with the school paper, she wondered whether students would find that sort of story interesting or not."

I deflated. "Oh. Okay."

"Then, she realized that since the thief was a real monster, that must be the, er, hook. Is that right? The hook?"

"Yes, that's right. Wow." Now that I had the go-ahead, I felt instantly nervous. I'd have to text Alex for advice.

"She and her husband, Dennis, always go to the Farmer's Kitchen for Sunday dinner. They finish at around two o'clock, and she wondered if you might want to interview them there at the restaurant."

My mind worked. Our church let out at eleven, which would allow for plenty of time to have lunch with my family and bike to the Farmer's Kitchen by two. "Yes! I can do that."

"Wonderful. Have fun and write a great article."

"Thanks so much, Mrs. Kreps."

"Call me Betty. Ciao, dear."

"Bye. I mean, ciao."

*   *   *   *   *

It wasn't hard to spot them in the Farmer's Kitchen. By two o'clock, the dining room was almost empty. Plus, I recognized them immediately. But my stomach lurched when I saw Susanne's still-bruised eye. She had done what she could to cover it with makeup, but it still didn't hide the greenish-blue bloom across her brow bone.

"Thank you so much for meeting me," I said. "I'm Ursula Spark from East River Christian School." I extended my hand to Susanne first, then to Dennis.

"Well, thank you for coming over here," Dennis said, twirling the handle of his coffee cup. "We're Sunday afternoon regulars, and we like to linger."

Susanne smiled. "Life gets so hectic, we like to slow down on Sundays."

"My family does, too," I said, taking the seat that Dennis indicated. "But that's kind of my natural speed. So, I guess I should say I like it when everyone else slows down with me."

Susanne thought this was charming. "I remember you and your friends, now, from the line at the Butler."

I nodded.

"Did your friend—the nervous one—have as hard a time as she thought?"

I pressed my lips together. I didn't want to tell her how Kaia and I had left Livvie cowering in the balcony while we chased after the attacker. "Well … "

The couple grew serious. Dennis' face darkened. "I think we were all more upset by the end of the evening than we expected."

"Yes," I said, and tried not to look at Susanne's black eye. "I'm just so sorry that happened to you."

Susanne gave a graceful half-shrug. "I suppose it was going to happen to someone."

"Uh. Well." I pressed the record button on the voice recorder app on my phone, then covered it lightly with one hand. "Is it okay if I record this?"

"Absolutely," she said, and Dennis nodded.

I scooted the phone a few inches toward closer to them. "I guess that's why I wanted to talk to you both. I mean, I'm not a very good reporter. In fact, my editor said I shouldn't tell you this, but it's my first real interview. I'm actually the art director. I was at the show that night to do some drawings and a movie review." Susanne tilted her head, but I blurted, "I can't stop thinking about it, you know? I keep wondering, why you, out of all those people?"

Dennis cleared his throat and waved to the waiter for more coffee, and Susanne reached her hand across the table and patted my arm. "Sometimes," she said, "these things happen. Bad things. Why do bad things happen to us? That's an old question, isn't it?"

I swallowed and nodded. "It's hard to answer."

Susanne smiled. "It's your article, and I don't want to influence you too much. But when you write it, I'd like to see you touch on forgiveness."

"Forgiveness?"

She glanced at her husband. "It's been harder for Dennis than for me. But that's strictly off the record."

"It's not easy to see some doofus in a mask deck your wife," he said, and gripped his coffee mug like he was twisting a valve shut. Maybe his anger valve.

"No," I agreed, unsure of what else to say. What had Alex told me? Keep them talking. "Betty Kreps said you got your purse back, though. That's good. And that nothing but your money was missing?"

"I'm afraid it was a very boring purse," Susanne joked. "I only had thirty dollars or so, some lipstick and my tablet computer."

I looked up from my notebook. "Oh? Mrs. Kreps said your credit cards were left, but she didn't mention a tablet. I'm surprised he left that."

"I'm *relieved* he left it. It's valuable on its own, but it means more to me than its replacement cost. I teach English at Arthur High, and I use it to track all my lessons. In fact, it belongs to the school. The administration gave them to us just this year. It's a

45

part of a new grading system we're using." She sighed. "I'm afraid if I lost it, *I'm* the one who'd be going to the principal's office. Do the teachers at your school use anything like that?"

My scalp tingled. "No, but I think they've been talking about it. Did your students know you were going to go see *Frankenstein* on Tuesday?"

"Well, I told them if they went and filled out a little worksheet, I'd give them some extra credit on their next test." She sighed. "I only saw two or three in attendance." She appealed to me. "That's why I volunteered for your interview. It's a delight to help a high school student with a writing assignment!"

I groaned. "And then I told you I wasn't a writer. Oh, no."

They laughed, and Susanne took a sip of her coffee. "Write it anyway. Make it a doozy of a debut. In fact, send it to me. That would almost make this whole thing worth it."

"Honestly, writing's not my strength. But I'll try." I wiggled my phone at her. "I can do voice-to-text, and then edit that. It's a lot easier for me."

"Have you ever worked with a reading teacher?" she wondered.

I nodded. "That's who got me started with voice-to-text."

She beamed. "Then I know your article will be good. Anyone who's willing to work hard will always figure things out."

Chapter Six

When I left the Farmer's Kitchen and stepped into the coolness of the October day, my head was buzzing. I got a hop-start onto my bike and mashed the pedals into a head wind. Good. I needed the shock of it just then. I played Susanne's words back, over and over, until I coasted into Kaia's driveway. Leaning my bike against the garage, I turned and leaped onto the porch, then gave the doorbell three quick presses.

"Hey, Ursula." Kaia's sister, Khloe, stepped aside to let me in. "Kaia's in her room."

Their family had a gift for organization. Every nook of their home was converted into a usable space, and they somehow managed to stay out of one another's way ... for the most part. The attic didn't house plastic storage tubs of Christmas decorations, like mine. Instead, it was lined with shelves, custom-made by Kaia's dad from shipping pallets and scrap lumber. The shelves were filled with books, jars of pencils and erasers, a ball of yarn, a spider plant, and a few canvas bins. And tucked into the far corner, beneath the sole skylight, was Kaia's sleek futon bed. I adored her room. It was, much like my friend, tidy and put-together.

She was seated at her small white desk, one leg drawn up into her chair. She glanced over her shoulder and yawned. "Hey."

"I just got through talking to Susanne, the lady from the theater."

"Oh?" Kaia straightened her leg and swiveled to face me. "How was she?"

"She's okay—really sweet and inspiring, actually. She's got this horrible black eye." I waved in the general direction of her temple. "But, listen."

"I'm listening."

"I think I can guess who did it."

*   *   *   *   *

Arthur High school, with its yellow-glazed brick, looked like a giant beehive. The students streamed like bees out of the buildings, as if the hive had been hit with a stick. How in the world could I pick any single bee out of a swarm?

Then I saw him. He had his backpack slung over one shoulder again, his head tilted to gaze at his cell phone. I drew my own phone from my pocket and fired off a text to him.

Hi.

He swiped a finger across the screen. He was still too far away for me to see his face.

Over here.

He stopped walking, then cautiously scanned the horizon. When it seemed like he was looking at me, I lifted one hand and raised it in such a big wave, it was impossible to miss. No turning back now. I was committed.

He glanced down at his phone again.

I texted him again and put my phone back into my coat pocket.

Wenzinger's?

He took a quick look around him, then slowly made his way toward where I stood leaning against my bicycle."What's up?" he asked.

"I hoped you might be free right now. Do you have a job? I don't even remember if I asked you."

"You didn't," he said. "I don't."

"Ah," I said, then felt stupid. Talking to him was like prying rusty nails out of a two by four——if I kept working at it, something might come loose but when it did the momentum usually threw me off balance.

"But," he said. "I've been thinking about getting one. Know anyplace?"

"I—no, not off the top of my head," I said. I was too nervous to think.

"Maybe Werzinger's has a newspaper I can buy to check out the job postings." He had to shorten his stride so I could keep up with him as he started down the sidewalk toward the restaurant.

I smiled. "Wenzinger's."

"Yeah. That place. Whatever."

I hopped on my bike and drifted along next to him. "If they don't have a paper, they'll at least have a burger."

He glanced at me. "How can you ride a bike in a skirt?"

I shrugged. "I've been wearing a school uniform for years; you get used to it."

"Do *you* have a job?"

"No." But I do have a boss, I thought, and imagined Alex hunkered over the light box or the copy machine.

"Do you want one?"

"Maybe in the summer. What I want more than anything is to get accepted into art college. Hey," I changed subjects, feeling weird about revealing too much to him. "What about Wenzinger's? Trying to get a job there, I mean?"

"Maybe." He was as distracted as ever but seemed to be thawing.

"Did you watch the movie yet?"

"Yeah."

I waited a few seconds until I couldn't stand it any more. "And?! What did you think?"

The wind lifted the hair off his forehead as we waited for the crosswalk signal. "It was … It's not at all like the book."

"I haven't read it."

"You should." He pulled his backpack open and drew out mangled paperback, then reached in again and grabbed the DVD. He tucked the disc between the pages and reached for the handlebar of my bike. "Here. You loaned me the movie. I'll loan you the book."

I let him steer while I studied the book cover. "You should keep this," I said, and this time it was me who avoided eye contact. "I'm a really slow reader. It might take me two years to finish it," I joked.

"That's okay; I don't need it back for a while."

"No, really," I said. "I have dyslexia. But if you think I should read it, I'll listen to the audiobook, okay?" I held the book out to him. "I can read. Not to sound defensive, but I want you to know that. It does take a little longer, though, and usually something else gets my attention before I can finish a long book that big. With audiobooks, I can listen to them while I do other things." I sighed. "I'm trying to get my grades up so I can get into Northwestern. A lot of artists are dyslexic, you'd think they'd be a little understanding at an art college but I don't want to take any chances. Sorry, I'll shut up about it. What do *you* want to do? After high school, I mean?"

I physically clenched my teeth so I'd stop talking. What was wrong with me? I usually didn't bring up my dyslexia if I could avoid it. Well, there it was. I guess this would be a test to see how he'd react. A lot of times, people think I'm dumb because I can't spell very well or can't see words they way they do. Then they feel sorry for me. At least I got ahead of the suspicion this time.

He took the book from me and was quiet for a minute. I braced myself for the usual questions people asked when I told them. Like whether I wrote letters backwards. But instead, he licked his lips and said, "I'd like to do something in film. I'm trying to make some videos to start a YouTube channel, but … " he shrugged. "I'm still figuring it out."

"That's so cool. Is that why you wanted to watch *Frankenstein*?"

He nodded. "It's like, always listed in the top films ever made, but I'd never seen it. I watched an interview with my favorite director, and he said it was a major influence, so … It was pretty amazing. The lighting was cutting edge when it was made, but now we have animation and computer-generated action scenes. I guess I was impressed that even though it's low-tech, it's still a really creepy movie. Boris Karloff's the man."

I nodded and slipped the disc into my tote. "At first I thought the sets were pretty hokey but then I got sucked in and felt like I was there. I loved the costumes. Her wedding dress? Unbelievable! So gorgeous. I drew it, like, five times."

"Is that why you're going to art school? You like to draw?" he asked, letting me have the handlebars again.

"Drawing is what I like the most." I loved how he said, 'going to art school,' not 'trying to get into art school'.

"Have anything with you?"

"What do you mean?" The gravel in Wenzinger's parking lot crunched beneath my tires.

"Any drawings that you'd let me see?"

"Oh. Yeah, probably. I have those dress sketches with me." I dismounted and snugged the front wheel into the bike rack, next to an English-racing-green road bike with rusty pedal cranks and a torn saddle. Just mentioning my sketchbook made my fingers itch to draw the bicycle. I'd draw it leaned against a huge maple tree, with a few brave leaves left on the branches. I sneaked a quick glance at Matt. His cheeks were flushed from the wind, one edge of his collar folded and sticking up out of the neck of his sweatshirt. Without thinking, I reached to smooth it like I would Leo's collar.

"What?" he asked, flinching away from me.

"It's—here. Sorry." I flipped the edge down and felt my own face warm. "I'll be right in, okay? I need to let my parents know where I am."

He nodded and went in.

I spun away from the building and sent Mom a quick text. Then I texted Kaia.

Forget the plan. Tell you later.

I slid into the booth. It was the same table I'd chosen a few nights earlier, when I was waiting for him to show up. My stomach flopped. This was not going the way I imagined, and I said a quick prayer for help.

52

Matt had found a newspaper and was spreading it out across the table. He was frowning. "Not much here," he said.

"How do you like Jewel Valley?"

"It's different," he said, as if he was used to giving that answer. Then, he looked up from the wanted ads. "I haven't gotten used to it at all."

"How long have you been here?"

He looked me in the eye for maybe the first time, ever. His eyes were gray. Not blue or hazel, but a serious gray. "I don't think it's going to work out."

"Give it some time," I heard myself saying. "When you get a job, make it through your first winter and see the spring? I think you'll like it."

"At home," he started, but grew quiet when the waitress came. She laid menus on the table. He waited until she took our drink orders and drifted away again. "At home, there was always so much going on, so much to get into, you know? And here … " He stared out the window at the dark green carpet of a rolling pasture. "Here, there are farms. A lot of farms."

"There's more than farms," I said, a little defensively.

"Like?" He turned back to me. His question seemed heavy, like it weighed more than the word itself.

Suddenly, to my horror, I felt a lump tightening in my throat and knew that unless I changed the subject soon, I would lose control and cry. I yanked my sketchbook out and flipped through pages until I found the sketches of Mae Clarke, the actress from the movie. I'd Googled her obsessively over the weekend. I pushed the notebook across the table and scanned the dining room for Molly, the waitress. She eventually came with our drinks, but Matt only studied the sketches. I ordered fries but he shook his head and Molly glided away.

I tapped my fingers on the tabletop a few times, then glanced at my phone. There was a text from Mom, asking me to be home by five-thirty. And one from Kaia:

Do you need me?

That made the tears prickle my eyes again. I needed a distraction, so I asked, "Well, what do you think?" Then I texted Kaia back that everything was fine.

"How long does it take you to do one of these?" he asked. "I mean, one like this?"

I blew out a breath. "I don't know, it depends if I'm getting it right or not. I'll take all the time I have. They're never really finished, you know? I usually just have to stop. Something else will get my attention and I move on."

"I can only draw stick figures," he muttered. He flipped a page back.

"I could teach you some hacks if you really wanted to. People think they're no good at drawing but a lot of it is just like everything else: practice."

"I don't think so," he said. "You're dyslexic with reading? I'm dyslexic with drawing. But that's what you should do for a summer job. Art lessons for kids.'"

"Could that work?"

"Yeah, definitely. At home, it was a big deal. Parents get sick of their kids when school's out."

"I never thought about that."

Molly landed a basket of fries on the table.

"Try it. I mean, look at these." He flipped another page back and froze. It was the sketch I'd done at the Butler, on the night of the movie.

"It's you," I said softly, "in the balcony."

It was as if I'd hit him in the gut with a bag of those Arthur

High School yellow bricks. His eyes were locked onto the paper, and a muscle in his jaw clenched and unclenched, working back and forth. His free hand curled into a fist. I saw the color drain from his face and he turned winter pale.

"What's wrong?"

"Nothing," he said in a low voice.

"I talked to her yesterday."

"Huh?"

As I looked at him across the well-worn tabletop of my favorite booth at my favorite hangout, I thought about what it would be like to move away from it all. Everything I knew and loved. I lost any courage I had scraped together to mention Susanne, and I veered in another direction. "Kaia, my friend. She was with me when I drew that." I flicked my index finger at the sketchbook. "You'll see more of her at the Butler."

He shrugged.

"Listen, you finish these, I have to go home. Mom's texting me." I slid the fries to him and scooted out of the booth, grabbing my tote and sketchbook and coat. "Just give the Valley a chance. I know it's—different. But it could grow on you."

He pulled the fries closer and stared at them then rewarded me with a quick glance before fastening his eyes on something out the window. "Doesn't matter. I never get a say in it anyway."

I handed Molly my money and hurried from the restaurant. Kaia waited for me at the bike rack. "You didn't confront him?"

I sighed. "No. I met him after school. We came here. I was going to tell him we knew who robbed Susanne, just like you and I planned. But, I don't know, we started to talk about things. I couldn't bring it up. I will. I *know* I will. But I started thinking about how it would feel to land in a town like the Valley, how disorienting it would be. And he was sad, Kai, really sad. The timing was all wrong. I felt it."

Kaia watched me while I spoke, and was silent for a few moments as we coasted our bikes from the lot. Finally she asked, "You felt it in your spirit?"

Had I felt it in my spirit? "I'm not sure. I prayed while I waited for him. But the things I prayed for … " I shook my head. "I prayed for the right words to trap him. I was proud, you know? Proud we've gotten this far. But the longer I made small talk, the worse I felt about it all."

"Then we need to give it some time."

I envied the firm conviction in Kaia's voice. It was the same advice I'd given Matt. "All I know is that I couldn't bring it up."

Kaia nodded.

"What about Livvie? Have you talked to her recently?"

"Not since yesterday," Kaia said. "You're right. Something is definitely bothering her."

"Any ideas?"

Kaia exhaled through her nose and leaned back in her chair. "I think she's freaking out."

"Yeah, but about what?"

"Does it have to be one single thing?" Kaia asked. "Her parents are freshly divorced and she doesn't know what that means yet. School is hard. She thinks she's bad at everything. And she wants a boyfriend to come along and fix it all."

"Jeesh, when you put it like that… We need to go get her right now."

Kaia smiled and picked up her coat. "Agreed."

We parked our bikes at my house then walked the short distance down Bluebird Street to Livvie's. The windows were dark. "Think she's home?" Kaia asked.

"When I texted her and said you were coming to my house, she said she was going to get caught up on some studying." I made a face. "Who voluntarily gets caught up on studying?"

"Suspicious." Kaia pressed the doorbell. "Better not mention the project."

"What project?"

"Our investigation."

"Oh. Right."

We waited but there was no answer. Kaia rang the bell and I sent another text. Nothing.

"How'd you figure out all that stuff about Livvie, earlier?" I asked as we walked back to my house. "You were like a psychic or something."

"I read some articles on the Focus On the Family website. I was supposed to be researching my persuasive essay."

Chapter Seven

"Hello?" Alex tapped his chewed-up pen on the side of the computer screen.

"Oh, my gosh, that's so disgusting," I cried, scooting away in the office chair.

"What?"

"Your pen! It's a chew toy! Now your spit germs are probably going to multiply and crawl all over the keyboard, so that—hold on, I have to write this down. That would make a really great GIF for the flu season reminder we're putting in next week's post." I pulled my sketchbook toward me and jotted the idea on the inside cover.

Alex waited until I was finished, then said, "I was trying to get your attention. You were zoned out and I asked you three times what you thought about the new lunch menu."

"Oh. Sorry. Uhm, don't care?"

"You've got to give me something, here."

"Really. I'm serious. I don't care about spaghetti versus penne. They're both pasta. I mean, it's a shape. I don't see what the big deal is."

"No," he said, coming around to lean on the edge of the desk and cross his arms in his most convincing editor's pose. "I mean about the Livvie problem."

"The Livvie problem?"

"Come on. You two are still having issues. It's pretty obvious."

I clenched my molars together. "It's not 'issues'."

"Well, something is going on. Don't hold back, you can tell ol' Alex."

I rolled my eyes to the ceiling. "Ol' Alex knows Ursula hates it when he speaks in the third person."

He held up his hands in surrender. "Okay, fine. Sit here and soak in your angst. I'll keep pretending there's someone else in the room when I ask you questions."

"Thank you." I turned back to the screen and worked with the graphics program, trying to get the logo to look just right. It was a job I took pride in, and I spent more time on it than I should. When I'd first started working on the blog late last year, it was just Alex and Mr. Lowe, and The Roar's logo was a generic clip art someone had found online. That was one of the first things I did, redesign the header and logo. And my efforts had paid off. Parents and businesses complimented the school on the website's sleek design all the time. It had even snagged me two freelance logo design jobs that I did in exchange for experience for my portfolio and gift certificates to Wenzinger's.

I loved reworking images with the design software. I could fine-tune to my heart's content. But I could easily get lost for hours at a time if I wasn't interrupted or if I forgot to set the alarm on my phone. Alex had discovered this. He was glad to leave me to my work while he was on his own project. But when he finished up before me, he would nearly always break my concentration.

"Leave the logo alone; it's fine."

"I'm smoothing this edge."

"It's fine! You've spent more time on that ridiculous logo than you have on all the other sketches put together."

"Exaggerating," I muttered.

"How's your article on the Butler robbery coming along?"

I pushed away from the screen and swung around again. "You know I'm a terrible speller, so even though I'm holding hands with voice-to-text and spell-check, I'll still need you to proofread it for me."

He made a small bow. "But, of course."

"It's harder and easier than I thought it would be."

"How do you mean?"

"The facts were easy to write. I didn't get choked up like I thought I would. But the things I left out are hard. Emotionally, I mean."

"Like?"

"Like, I think about Susanne and Dennis going out, waiting in line, being so happy, looking forward to seeing the movie. And then, just a few minutes later, their whole lives changed. They'll never go to the Butler—or any movie—without thinking about that night."

"Maybe so."

"Is this really what you want to do when you grow up?"

He straightened his slender shoulders and drew himself to his full height. "I am grown up."

"I'm serious."

"You already know the answer," he said, twirling his chewed pen in one hand. "Yes, more than anything."

"How can you want to do *this* more than anything? How can you stand it? Look at all the sadness and the hurt that live in our little town. You want to chase stories all over the world. How will you keep from … drowning in it all?"

"The truth never makes me feel like I'm drowning," he said, his voice low and even. "It's not knowing the truth that feels—"

He paused for the right word. "Dark. Wrong. But, you're right, uncovering the truth isn't always pretty."

I snorted.

"It's still more important than anything. It shows us who we are."

"How? How does this story show us who we are? I'm more confused than I've ever been."

"It shows who you are," he said, and glanced away, focusing on the computer screen. "You care about what happened to a woman you barely know and you want to make things right for her. I can see you perfectly."

I felt my face flush and I turned to the monitor, too. "Stop being nice to me. It throws me off."

He smirked. "Get the article finished. You've got two days."

That sounded more like Alex. I let my breath out. "Fine."

"I need those illustrations, too," he said, and left the office.

*　　　　*　　　　*　　　　*　　　　*

"I've got plans," Livvie said, and pushed her locker shut.

"What plans?" I asked.

"They're kind of private."

"Oh," I said, stung. "Listen, I'm sorry if I did something to upset you. I didn't mean to. Please tell me. Is it because of the—this thing with the Frankensteins?"

"Nope. You're good." She started down the hallway.

I had to trot to keep up with her, and struggled to keep my voice low so we wouldn't be overheard. "Then what's up? I don't understand."

She stopped walking and blinked at me. "People grow up. You

can't think that we'll stay the same forever."

It was like the shiny tile floor dropped out from beneath me. "What?"

She rolled her eyes and heaved a huge sigh. "I need some space, okay? You don't have to know every single thing I do every minute of every day." She softened her tone slightly. "Look, maybe I'll call you or something. But I've got things to do now."

She walked around me and left me there, standing alone by the lockers.

*   *   *   *   *

"She said that?"

I blew my nose. "Yep."

Kaia narrowed her eyes. "What's going on?"

"You tell me. You're the wise one."

She tilted her head. "No, I'm not."

I blew my nose again and rubbed my blurry eyes. "It's been a rough day."

"Probably not as rough as Livvie's," she murmured, tapping her fingertips lightly on her jaw.

"No! No, you didn't see her. She's not upset at *all*. She's just annoyed by me."

"Does that sound like her?"

I threw up my hands. "No. I feel like Livvie is gone."

"Where's Livvie?" She shook her head. "That's the wrong question."

Jeesh, she sounded just like Alex. "Okay, then what's the right question?"

Kaia frowned. "Oh, this is bad … "

"What?"

"The question is: why doesn't she want her closest friends around right now? What doesn't she want us to see?"

*   *   *   *   *

"Mom?"

She glanced up from the sink. "Hm?" She saw my red eyes and Kaia's grim face. "What happened?"

"We're worried about Livvie."

Mom dried her hands and put an arm around us both. "I know."

I shook my head. "No. We think she might want to hurt herself."

Mom's eyes widened, and she listened as we confessed our suspicions. "I see. Where is she now?"

"We're not sure," said Kaia. "She wouldn't tell us."

She nodded. "Okay. Try not to worry, but keep praying." She plucked her purse from the kitchen chair and slung her coat over her shoulders.

"What are you going to do? Can we come?"

Mom smiled reassuringly at us. "I think it would help most for you to stay here for now. Try not to worry," she said again. She went out the front door, shutting it behind her with a soft click.

I let my breath out with a whoosh. "I hope she finds her."

Kaia nodded. "She will."

"I hope we did the right thing."

Kaia didn't respond.

It was after ten o'clock when Mom slipped into the house. I was folded on the couch across from Dad, but I felt like a bundle of nerves. Kaia had to be home at eight, but I promised I'd message her when I knew anything.

"This will be okay," Kaia said, giving me a quick hug. It was a sign of the depth of her feelings on the matter; she was not a hugger.

"Is she alright?" I asked, rising to my knees on the couch and twisting to keep Mom in sight.

Leo was in bed, but likely eavesdropping if he was still awake. Mom kept her voice soft. "She's fine. Everything is okay. You should go to bed and get some rest for tomorrow." She reflexively checked her wristwatch.

"No way!" I whispered. "I can't sleep now; I'm too freaked out. What happened?"

Mom shed her coat and draped it over the back of the couch, then came to perch next to me. "Livvie will tell you all about it when she's ready. That's what we decided. You have to trust us both on this."

"I don't believe it, you have to tell me! At least something!"

But Mom only shook her head. "I can't, Little Bear. Not tonight."

"Mom, she's not talking to me. She's not going to tell me *anything*! You have to help me fix this."

Dad hit the mute button on the remote control. "You can't fix everything. That's Someone Else's job, isn't it?"

"You guys!" I wailed. "I came to you because I needed your help, not to be shut out even more!"

"Trust is hard," said Dad. "Welcome to adult life."

I ran upstairs before I said something that would get me grounded.

*   *   *   *   *

My mood spilled over into reality. I moved through my classes like a robot. Livvie was absent. Alex hovered. Mr. Lowe watched me from the corner of his eye during algebra II.

At the three-thirty bell, I zipped my coat, slung my tote over my shoulder, and burst out of school into the fresh air. For the first time that day, I felt like I could breathe, and I took several big gulps. Unlocking my bike, I threw a leg over the top tube and stared down the drive. Kaia had her piano lesson this afternoon. And, besides, with no new information, what was there to do but sit together and worry about Liv?

I pulled my phone out and found Matt's number.

Busy?

He responded quickly.

No.

Find a job?

Not yet.

Wenzinger's?

Be there in ten.

He was already in my favorite booth when I walked in. I crossed the dining room and sank into the vinyl seat. "Hi," I said.

He appraised me. "What's wrong?"

"It's just—" I shook my head and felt close to tears again. I pressed my fingertips against my eyes.

"Hey."

"I'm okay."

"I can see that."

"Sorry," I said, and gave him a shaky smile. I yanked a napkin from the dispenser and dabbed my nose. "I'm good."

He watched me closely.

I sighed and tapped the tabletop lightly with my knuckles.

"You know."

It wasn't a question. I lifted my eyes to meet his, and, for a moment, we said nothing. Finally, I nodded. He looked away.

"But," I said, waving at my damp eyes, "this is something else."

He frowned. "What do you mean?"

"I mean, I'm not trying to guilt you. I didn't ask you to come here so I could cry and make you feel guilty."

"Why did you?" His voice took a hardened to a sharp edge.

I swallowed. "I was going to talk to you about it the other day," I said, "but I couldn't."

"Why not?"

My mouth was suddenly dry, horribly dry, and I looked for a waitress. They were all busy. "You seemed so sad."

"So you felt sorry for me?"

I squeezed my hands together. Where was this going? I shook my head. "It just didn't seem like the right time."

"And now?"

"I didn't think now would be, either," I said.

"Just wanted a shoulder to cry on?" he sneered.

"What? No. I didn't mean to—look, I wanted some company, okay, but I didn't—"

"Just get to the point." He leaned back in the booth, and I saw the same person from the alley behind the Butler.

"Matt … "

He waited.

"Okay," I said. "Why didn't you tell us that you knew Susanne from Arthur?"

"Because it's none of your business."

I sighed. "I know it wasn't your idea."

He stared out the window.

I watched him clench his jaw, and felt irritation crawl up my spine. "I guess you've probably seen her black eye by now?"

He smirked.

"She told me that she forgives the thief."

"Great. What a hero." He moved to grab his backpack.

"You know she didn't deserve that."

"So, what, now you're going to preach to me, because you go to a Christian school? Forget it."

"This is between you and—"

"Just leave it, okay? If she doesn't care anymore, and the police don't care, why should you?"

"Because it's the truth," I said. "The truth shows us who we are."

"Wow," he scoffed, and started to leave.

"You don't have to go," I said.

He looked incredulous. "I absolutely do. You go on and on about truth and forgiveness, but you don't care about *actual* people. You think you know me well enough to say I looked sad to you? What do you know about my life?"

"That's not fair—"

"Life's not fair," he said and grabbed his backpack. "Everybody knows that." He got up and left.

Chapter Eight

"Come in."

I peeked around the door.

"Come on in," Mr. Lowe repeated, and waved me to take a seat in one of the chairs in front of his desk. "What's up?"

I perched on the edge of the nearest chair. "I have a problem."

Lowe lifted his gaze from his paperwork and looked at me over the tops of his gold-rimmed glasses. "What sort of a problem?"

"A moral dilemma." That was what Kaia said when she had a huge decision to make. It felt like the right words for my situation.

He smiled but it quickly faded. "What's wrong?"

I sighed. "I wish I had cash for every time someone asked me that this week," I muttered. "Okay, if I knew someone had committed a crime, would I have to—" I held up a hand as his expression changed. "Listen, it's not me and it's no one who goes to school here."

Lowe shook his head. "That's not what I was going to say."

"Oh."

"I was going to say that as a principal, there are certain things I'm obligated to tell the police."

"You are? I didn't know that. What kind of things?"

"Why don't you tell me and I'll let you know if we're heading into legally-obligated territory."

"Right. Okay. So, the victim has already forgiven. The police aren't actively investigating, and there's no real risk anymore. And, I'm pretty sure if I tell the truth, I'm going to lose a friend, and cause more of a mess than there already is."

"I see."

"And Livvie! I'm so worried about her! Do you know where she's been? My parents won't tell me."

"Bound by privacy."

"That's lame," I accused. Lowe let us talk to him that way when we were in his office. If I'd said that in class, I'd get detention or sent home.

He shrugged. "Everyone's got a right to privacy."

"Can you at least do something about Alex? He's on my back to get this article done."

"Aren't deadlines a part of every publication?"

I sighed. "I just need some advice, here. My life's a dumpster fire."

"Okay. First off, have you prayed?"

"Of course." I still felt a little convicted by his question, though. Prayer was hard; I get distracted so easily, it feels like my mind wanders before I ever finish praying about just one thing.

"Good. Next we go to the Bible? What does the Bible say about your moral dilemma? The Word is our moral absolute."

I searched my mind. "I don't know. I'm drawing a blank."

"Well, you might think it's cliché, but you can still ask, 'What would Jesus do'?"

I remembered the sermon from my church a couple of weeks ago. People had dragged a woman to Jesus and wanted him to carry out immediate justice. They were thirsty for blood and punishment. I remembered that he took his time, wrote something in the dirt on the ground, and extended mercy instead. In fact, I'd been really preoccupied with what he'd written in the dirt. Was Jesus doodling? Of course I focused on that idea! But the point was, he didn't allow the circumstances to rush him. And in the end, he'd won a follower instead of leading an execution.

"He would know the perfect words to say. He'd turn it all around and make it right," I murmured. "I can't *do* that. I can't even write without voice-to-text and spell-check."

Lowe smiled. "And Moses stuttered. Jeremiah was just a kid. Gideon was a wimp. Don't forget, the only thing you have to bring to the battle is yourself."

*　　　*　　　*　　　*　　　*

"She'll get over it soon, I'm sure," Alex said, stretching out on the library floor. He twisted and reached above him to slip a book back into its spot on the shelf. "What's the longest you two have ever gone without speaking?"

"Well, we're speaking. We have to, in a school this size."

"You know what I mean. What's the longest argument you've had?" He slapped his hands on the tile floor and pushed himself up. He came to the round table where I sat and pulled out a chair.

"I don't know."

"That can't be true," he said.

I sighed. "I guess it was two years ago. We had a fight."

"About what?"

"You're doing it again."

"What?"

"Grilling me."

He raised his hands. "Hey. I'm an interested friend, here, is there anything wrong with that?"

"Since when?" I asked.

He pouted. "That hurts."

"I'll bet."

"We've been in class together since fourth grade! If you don't want to tell me what the fight was about, just say so. No reason to attack."

I knew he was joking, but he managed to look so offended, I decided to tell him. Livvie wouldn't like it, but I didn't like how she was treating me. "It was about Kaia."

"Kaia?"

"She thought I liked Kaia more than her and she felt left out."

"Did you? And do you?"

"Of course not. They're apples and oranges."

He seemed amused. "And what are you?"

I stuck out my lower lip and considered. "Right now, I feel that I am rhubarb."

"That's pretty harsh. I'd at least say you're pear."

"Thanks. That means a lot to me."

"Don't mention it."

I glanced toward the library windows again. "I don't think she trusts me anymore, and I'm afraid she never will again." Once I said it, I wanted to pull the words back. I wanted them to be false. But I *was* afraid.

Alex shook his head. "Yes, she will. You've been friends since we were all little kids. People can't make new friends like that kind. They're not replaceable."

"You're right, I guess. I still don't know what to do now, though."

A light flicked on. "What are you two doing in here? You're supposed to be in the lunchroom." Mrs. Murga dumped her stack of folders for computer class onto the table nearest the door. She looked suspiciously at us, and pointed a finger at Alex. "Him, I expect to be sneaking around in here. But what are you up to, Ursula?"

"I'm hiding out," I said, resting my chin in my hand. "I didn't know he'd be in here."

She pursed her lips while she fished in her briefcase. "Well, as long as you're *both* here, help me pass out these worksheets."

*　　　*　　　*　　　*　　　*

I handed the flash drive to Kaia. "It didn't take as long as I thought it would."

She turned the drive over in her palm then pocketed it. "Nice gesture."

We'd decided to write and illustrate a picture book for Livvie. Over text messages, we came up with the idea, and I'd spent the night before scanning my illustrations into Buzzy's file system, then formatting them for Kaia. Now she had to do her part—write the story. "A card didn't seem big enough. Besides, I need to feel like I'm *doing* something."

"Praying *is* doing something."

"You know what I mean."

"Livvie knows we love her. That and prayer are the biggest things we can do."

"I can't be all serene like you, though."

Her brows lifted. "You think I'm serene?"

"Totally. You never let things bother you. I really wish I was more like that."

"I wish I was more like *you*."

72

I laughed. "That's crazy. Why?"

Kaia shrugged. "You always know what to say, and then you say it. No one ever has to wonder what you're feeling. You're … open."

"Isn't that the same as moody?"

She snorted. "No."

"But you're an actor! Can't you just act? If you want to be more open, you could *act* open."

"Playing a role isn't something you should get in the habit of doing in your real life," Kaia said. "Acting is pretend."

"But you're all—" I waved my hands in the air. "—mysterious. And so cool."

"Too mysterious, I think."

"You mean Blake?"

She looked surprised but nodded. Her cheeks darkened.

"If you wanted, I could talk to him, maybe, and see—"

She held up a hand. "Thanks, but no. I'm fine with the suffering for now."

"Okay, whatever. Just saying. Let me know and I'll start another investigation."

She smiled, then grew serious. "What about the investigation we're working on now? Isn't it time to wrap it up?"

I crossed my arms and gripped my elbows tight. "'It is never right to do wrong to do right.'"

"Deep, but which part do you mean?"

"I have no idea. I know the right thing is to get justice for Susanne and Dennis. But, when I wonder about taking what we know and going to the police, all I can think about is Matt. He'll never speak to me again."

"Is that so terrible?" she asked.

"It shouldn't be. We don't really know each other."

"But it is."

"Yeah, it kind of is. I feel like more is resting on this than the purse snatching. He thinks we're judging him because we go to a Christian school."

"Christian homeschool." She could never keep from correcting anyone on the topic.

"And," I pointed out, "we don't really know the motive, not really. Shouldn't we do a little more fact finding?"

Kaia gave me one of her long looks. "If you feel like it's important, then look into it further."

"Thanks."

She patted the flash drive in her pocket. "I've got enough to keep me busy for a while, anyway."

*   *   *   *   *

Mrs. Kreps beamed at us from the ticket booth and waved toward a guy with shaggy brown hair who sat in the far corner of the booth, staring at his phone screen. "Got a security guard," she crowed.

I smiled and gave her the thumbs up. He didn't look like a very intimidating security guard. But Kaia and I didn't stop to chat. Instead, we made our way to the stage. She'd texted me that Matt had joined the Butler Brats and that he was helping with early rehearsals. Of course, I pedaled right over.

Clusters of parents were hanging out in the house, with a few rowdy kids playing hide-and-seek in the balcony. The acoustics carried their voices, magnifying them, so it seemed that the theater was full. Teens bustled on the stage and from behind the curtain, and a ballerina in jeans did a few pirouettes, toppling and giggling at the end. Opening night for the Nutcracker was in a month.

I followed Kaia backstage, where several guys and a girl were coiling ropes and sound cables and sorting them into piles. Matt straightened from his crouched position, and I got to watch his expression change as he recognized us. Like the weather, he went from partly cloudy to thunderstorm in an instant. Wonderful. I braced myself and stepped around a mound of thick nylon rope so I could speak without being overheard. Kaia crossed to the far edge of the work area and struck up a conversation with the other members of the crew, so I could draw Matt away. If he agreed to be drawn away.

"Hey, can I talk to you for a few minutes? I won't waste your time."

Matt glanced over his shoulder, where his uncle stood talking to another man. The two surveyed the evening with obvious pride, watching young people rush around and joke with friends. "I guess so. You'll probably blackmail me if I tell you two to get away from me."

I tried not to cringe. "Kaia is here to work," I said, managing to keep most of my defensiveness from oozing out. "I'm on your side. Kaia's on my side. So help me out. Give me something to go on."

He dropped the end of the cable he was holding and it hit the waxed wooden floor with a bang. Kaia shot a quick look in my direction, but I shook my head and followed Matt to the alley.

He rubbed the back of his neck. "You've poked your nose far enough into this whole thing to figure out who did it."

"You were surprised that night when you heard me say there were three Frankensteins in the main theater. But it was more than that; you already knew who the fourth Frankenstein was. Your brother."

His agitation bubbled up. "You might be on my side, but I'm

not on yours. I'm always on *his* side, even if I'm the only one. So, do what you have to do, and get it over with. I already gave him a heads up, and he left town."

My mouth dropped open. "I didn't think that—"

"That he might already have a record? No. You didn't think."

"Hey!" I crossed my arms. "Maybe if you'd explain why he felt like he had to punch a teacher to change his grade, I'd understand. What's worth making her remember that every time she goes out with her husband, now?"

Hurt passed across his face before he could stop it. "He didn't mean to do that. It was a reflex when she wouldn't let go of the purse. He only meant to push her back, but in the mask, he couldn't see..." His shoulders sagged and he fell quiet. Then he said, "Steve got us both costumes to help out that night. But Robbie didn't want to go. So when I heard you count three other guys, I knew it had to be him. And, yeah, Steve knew, too, and covered for him." He scoffed. "Not because we're family, but just so he doesn't have to be embarrassed in front of his friends at the Butler. Everyone has let it go but you."

We faced one another in the dim yellow light, our breath rising in clouds of steam. He rubbed the edge of his closed fist against the rough bricks, scuffing his knuckles. A whiny car drove past, speakers booming. Finally, he said, "Ursula, please. Don't do this."

"Talk to me," I said, my voice wavering. "I don't understand."

He leaned against the building. "Our mom's in jail. We stayed with my grandma for a while, but it didn't work. Robbie got in trouble, and he flunked his last year at our high school. So we came to live with Mom's brother, Steve." He nodded toward the building. "And it's better. But he's still flunking English. That's all he needs to pass, and then he'll graduate in the spring. Sad story, huh?"

"But he can't just force his way like that," I said softly.

"Yeah, I know," Matt snapped. "He's really depressed about it. He's changed. But, you're going to throw him in jail, I guess, so what does it matter?"

I wouldn't take that bait. Instead, I asked, "You believe him?"

He faltered, and I could see that Robbie had made other promises before. "Yeah."

I knew I had to be careful from here. "Do you—have you ever seen someone who's able to make up their mind to change, and just do it?"

"People can change if they want to bad enough."

"The only time I've seen anyone really change is when they have outside help."

"Wait, wait." He held up a hand and smirked. "I see where this is going. Jesus, right?"

"It just seems that—"

"Like everyone who knows Jesus does the right thing?"

"No, I didn't say that."

"When Robbie and I needed help, how many Jesus people do you think stepped up to lend a hand?"

"How many other people did?" I countered.

"Okay, so there's no difference, right?"

"I can only speak for myself, and I'm trying to help you both right now. And it's because of Jesus. So quit being a jerk and let's think of a way out of this."

His eyebrows lifted and he opened his mouth to say something, then shut it again. He took a deep breath. "Look, you're a good person, probably, okay? But you don't know what it's like to be us. What real problems have you ever had? Thanks for the offer, but we'll figure this out like we always have—by ourselves."

He pushed off the wall, and banged on the door. A stage hand opened it, and Matt waved me inside, then went back to his ropes.

Kaia kept her eyes on us. She finished duct-taping a cable to the floor, then circled around to meet me. She studied my face, then sighed. "Now what?"

Chapter Nine

"Thanks for meeting me again," I said.

Susanne smiled across the table at me, the corners of her eyes creasing. There was the faintest tinge on her brow bone now, the only visible trace of a trying couple of weeks. The waitress came to take our drink orders. "I'll have a cola with lemon," Susanne said, then winked at me. "I feel like a splurge. I love Wenzinger's. It always makes me feel like a little girl again."

The waitress smiled as she jotted on her notepad, then fixed her eyes on me. "The usual?"

I nodded. "Thanks."

Susanne said, "You must come here often."

"Pretty much every other day, I think. I blow my allowance on fries and art supplies." I pushed my still-closed menu to the edge of the table.

"It's a lovely place. How's the article going?"

"It's almost finished. But I was hoping you could help me with the ending."

"Oh?"

"Yeah. I hit a dead end."

Starting at the beginning, I told her everything I knew about the Frankenstein purse-snatcher. Sensing the gravity of our conversation, the waitress landed our drinks as softly as feathers and flitted away again. I had to look at the place mat for the hard parts, but when I finished, I raised my eyes to Susanne's dark blue ones and waited.

She pulled her bubbling cola to her and took a sip, then another. She pushed the glass away from her, then folded her hands. "And you were able to find all this out yourself? When the police couldn't find anything?"

I cleared my throat. "Well, Kaia and I. And, you know, the police weren't looking. They thought someone heard about the costumes and snuck in, then took your purse for the money."

Susanne dabbed the corner of her sore eye with the napkin. "I haven't told anyone this, but the money was returned."

"Really?"

She nodded. "Two days ago. It was in my mailbox at school, in an envelope. I could have checked the closed circuit camera footage and maybe seen who returned it, but … " She dabbed her eye again. "I knew, then, it was a student, and I really didn't want to know which one."

"I'm sorry," I said quickly. "I didn't know."

Susanne shook her head. "No, sweetheart. Please don't be. I'm so glad to know the whole story."

"I thought it should be your decision. You're the one who was hurt."

"It never—never once—occurred to me that this was about school grades." She chuckled and took another long sip. "I should have known. Students are so savvy with technology. It took me two weeks just to learn how to turn that awful tablet on."

I smiled, but felt sad in the pit of my stomach. "I hope it makes you feel a little better, in some ways."

Susanne took a deep breath. "It makes me feel better to see young people who care," she said. "I worry about the world, some days, because I see so much selfishness. But then I find you, and Kaia, and Robbie's brother."

I looked up. "Matt?"

Susanne nodded firmly. "Him. He has such love and loyalty to his brother."

I swallowed. "He doesn't think anyone else would ever help them."

Susanne leaned across the table and whispered, "Let's prove him wrong."

*   *   *   *   *

Wednesday morning was the sort of clear, frosty fall morning that I adored. The sky was a smooth azure, except for a few tendrils of lavender clouds low on the horizon.

"It's chilly. Why don't I drop you off?" Mom asked from the kitchen as she topped off her travel mug with coffee and smoothed her skirt.

"No, thanks. I'd rather ride. It looks amazing out there."

"Okay, but don't forget your gloves and earmuffs."

I waved my gloves. "Got 'em. 'Bye."

As I pedaled the two miles to school, I soaked in all of the morning I could, recharging myself with beauty. The rosy light shone against the branches of the trees, some of them bare now, changing them to gleaming gold. Smoke and steam rose in wispy trails from the rooftops, then dissipated in the clear, cold air. It smelled like dry concrete and wood smoke.

It was moments like this, when my heart was so full it felt like it was squeezing out of my ribcage, that made me wonder how anyone missed God. Here He was, all around me, and I felt Him

81

so close. I knew then, somehow, everything would work out.

I coasted to the bike rack and locked my bike, threading the helmet straps through the lock and snapping them together. I fluffed my hopeless hair and slipped my ear muffs into my tote, then started to the school.

There was a group of students clustered around the side entrance. Kyle turned and saw me approaching, then their talk hushed as they parted to let me get to the door. I frowned.

A paper was taped to the glass door. The corners flapped gently in the breeze. It took me a moment to recognize my own sketch of Mrs. Murga. It was one I'd done a few weeks earlier, when I was supposed to be editing the cells in my spreadsheet during computer class. But it had been edited. Someone had carefully added a mustache to Mrs. Murga's face. It was true that the teacher had a line of fine, pale hairs on her upper lip. But I would never have drawn those.

Behind me, someone snickered. "Nice," one of the senior boys said.

I ripped the paper down and stuffed it into my tote. "This wasn't me," I said over my shoulder, summoning as much indignation as I could. I ran to the bathroom and tossed the tote onto the counter then yanked out my sketchbook and flipped through it. Several pages had been carefully ripped out. Not one page. Several.

My mind racing, I leaned against the sink. Ella Singleton came into the restroom and did a double-take.

"Uhm," she said, smothering a smile, "Mr. Lowe's looking for you."

"I did NOT do these!" I said, waving the crumpled paper.

"Well, they're pretty much everywhere," she said, with a little more sympathy. "Someone did a good job setting you up." She went into one of the stalls.

Lowe was waiting for me in the lunchroom. He nodded toward his office, and I tried to ignore the ripple of laughter from a corner table as I finished my walk of shame across the tiled floor. I sank into the chair as he closed the door behind me.

"This wasn't me," I said, dropping my face in my hands. How many more times would I have to say it?

"I assumed it wasn't completely your work," he said, sitting down behind his desk. He propped his elbows on the desk blotter. "But you can't tell me someone can imitate your drawings *that* well."

I shook my head and took a deep breath. I felt a little better knowing he believed I didn't do the worst, but my heart still banged in my chest. "The sketches are mine, but someone did an awful thing to the one of Mrs. Murga."

Lowe pressed his lips together, then said, "Why did you sketch her in the first place?"

I felt my face go red. "I was supposed to be working on my spreadsheet, but my eyes were going crossed staring at those little black and white boxes, so, you know, I goofed off a little bit. I wasn't making fun of her, I promise. I just draw people sometimes to practice, especially their hands, but she was the only one standing up that I could look at, so … " I trailed off because the lump in my throat choked my voice.

"In the future, I would suggest staying focused on your work," he said mildly, and scooted his chair. Then I noticed the stack of mid-weight drawing papers on the corner of the desk.

"Oh, no," I said, my eyes locked on the pile. "Are those … ?"

He nodded. "Whoever your fan is has quite an insight. I especially like the double-chins on my portrait."

The tears came then. Humiliation washed over me. "I am so, so sorry. I doodled you last week in devotions."

He handed me the box of tissues from his book shelf. "I hope you got the gist of the sermon."

"I did," I bawled. "I promise. It helps me listen, sometimes, to keep my hands moving. You probably don't believe me, but it's true. You know I draw everything. Even when I study for a test." I sobbed, and blew my nose. "Last night I drew a stupid caffeine molecule, like, a hundred times."

He smiled. "You work hard at school, Ursula. I know you do. Try to calm down."

"It's so *embarrassing*." I dabbed my eyes. "Please send me home; I can't face everyone after this."

"Just take some time, don't worry so much. No one's angry. They didn't expect this from you any more than I did. But do you have any idea who might be a little, shall we say, perturbed at you right now?"

"No," I said. Then my heart sank. My tears dried up with the shock of realization. "Yes."

From his expression, I knew he had already figured it out. He just didn't want to be the one to tell me.

I hurried to smooth it over. "You can't do anything about this, though. At least, not right now. So wait a while, okay? She's been having a really rough time."

He sighed. "Didn't you come in here a few days ago to ask what to do when you knew someone had done something wrong?"

I deflated. "This is different."

He stood and put his hands in his pockets. "I'll see what I can do. But you know it's not right for us to ignore it. Go to class, now."

I looked up at him. "I'm too embarrassed."

"You didn't do anything wrong," he said. "Except, maybe, check out and sketch when you should have been paying attention."

I shook my head. "I don't think I can do it. Can't I just hide out in the janitor's closet today? I'll polish the trophies. Anything."

He rubbed his face. "How's your article coming along?"

*   *   *   *   *

Alex found me. "Hey."

"This is pretty good," I murmured, looking up from C. S. Lewis's *Out of the Silent Planet*, which I'd pulled off the shelf solely because of the cover design. I had to concentrate so hard on reading the first few pages, it was the perfect distraction.

He sank to the floor next to me. "Lowe said you've been working on the blog all day."

I nodded. "Just the article. Got a few class assignments done, too. Pretty productive morning."

He watched me. "That was wrong, using your special talent against you."

I winced. "It was … I don't think she meant it."

He looked away.

"It's like Frankenstein. My creations came to life and got away from me, then started hurting people."

"I think your creations had a little help, Dr. Frankenstein."

I cleared my throat. "Is she still here?"

He shook his head. "Sent home."

"How long?"

He shrugged. "We don't know yet."

"Come on. You had to have heard something."

"Ursula."

"Please. I'd text her but I know she won't answer."

He sighed. "Ella says it's three days."

"Ugh. That seems a little harsh."

"She'll be fine. And she deserves it."

"It doesn't feel that way."

"Stop blaming yourself. She's lucky to have a friend like you," he said. "Go eat something."

I waved an empty granola bar wrapper at him. "I'm good, thanks."

He stood and turned to leave.

"Alex?"

"Yeah?"

"Is Mrs. Murga mad at me?"

He hesitated. "She's a little mad. But not at you. Tomorrow no one will even mention it."

I scoffed. "Right."

"The day's half over," he said, and walked toward the door to the lunchroom.

"Not even close," I muttered. I waited until he was gone and sent Kaia a text.

Is it ready?

The reply came seconds later.

Almost.

Will it be done tomorrow?

Yep.

Send it.

Gotcha.

*　　　　*　　　　*　　　　*　　　　*

The scarlet glow of Wenzinger's sign had never looked so beautiful to me as it did at that moment. I stood at the bike rack after locking up my ride, and watched people go in and out. I tried to steady myself, but my heart pounded painfully. What a difference a few hours made! This morning, I had been blissed-out with beauty and assurance. Now, my gut was stabbed with doubt and pure, sharp fear. I leaned against the bike rack and tried to slow my breath.

I breathed a raggedy prayer for help as I crossed the gravel lot.

And then, Mr. Lowe's words came back to me: "Moses stuttered. Jeremiah was just a kid. Gideon was a wimp." I straightened my shoulders. I had everything I needed. I smoothed my khaki uniform skirt and scrunched my helmet hair.

When I opened the door of the diner, a burst of laughter and warm golden light washed over me. Feeling strengthened, I took a deep breath of fry-scented air and went to my standard booth. I started to sit facing the door, then changed my mind and switched sides. I drew my sketchbook from my tote and then fished out the pencil pouch.

I was nearly a third of the way into a drawing of a spaceship hovering over a row of adorable Victorian houses when, out of the corner of my eye, I noticed a pair of jeans. I looked up, pencil poised above the vapor trail from the spaceship, and blinked.

Matt's eyebrows were drawn into a knot. "What's that for?" He sat opposite me, and stuffed his hands into his hoodie pocket.

"I was just messing around," I said, flipping the notebook closed.

All the fight seemed to have gone out of him. I tapped out a quick text and hit send. He waved the waitress away, then refocused. "What do you want, now?" he asked.

"How's Robbie?"

He frowned. "Fine."

"You should tell him to come back."

"Why would I do that?"

I heard the door open and close behind me, and realized that maybe I should have taken the seat facing the door. I watched Matt's eyes widen, then crystallize with anger. Anger toward me.

Susanne walked to the table, blocking him from the door. There was the fire escape, but running out that door would sound the alarm. She approached slowly, and pointed at the vinyl seat next to him. "May I?" she asked.

He stiffly scooted over, glaring at the salt and pepper shakers. Two bright pink spots appeared on his cheeks. I clenched my hands into fists on my lap. It was terrible to watch. Please, God, let this work.

"Matt, I know your brother, but I haven't met you. I'm Susanne. I'll likely have you in my class for English next year."

With great effort, he looked at her and nodded.

"Ursula has been very worried about you," she said.

He leveled a look of hatred across the table. "I don't need that."

"But I think I should have some say in it. What do you think?"

The muscle in his jaw was working overtime. He shrugged.

"I think, if Robbie regrets this whole series of choices—and I believe he does, since he returned the money—"

Matt's head jerked up. It was, apparently, a revelation to him.

"—he needs to prove it." Susanne let her words sink in.

"He can't be arrested again," Matt said in a near-whisper. "He'll go to jail."

"That's not what I had in mind."

He shook his head. "Then what?"

"I want to help him graduate."

Matt licked his lips. "How? He's failing and needs your class."

"It's not too late. I'll stay after school every day and tutor him until he makes it. But he has to come back, and show up to school."

He searched her face. "Why would you do that?"

Susanne smiled. "Someone did it for me, once."

He sat up straight and looked between Susanne and me. "What's the catch?"

"No catch," I said. "Just some help."

He looked back at the table, then nodded. "I'll tell him."

Susanne stood to let him out.

"Thank you." Matt extended his hand. "Very much."

"You're quite welcome," she said, and shook his hand. "I hope to hear from you tomorrow. You know where my room is?"

He nodded. "I'll find it." They headed for the door.

I threw the money for my hot chocolate on the table and grabbed my coat, following them into the parking lot. Susanne gave me a quick hug and waved at Matt. "We'll talk soon," she said, giving him a meaningful smile.

"Bye." He lifted a hand as she got into her car and pulled onto the street.

"I'd better go home," I said, fumbling with the lock on my bike. "I sort of didn't get to any of my classes today. Probably should check on my homework."

"I guess I owe you an apology."

"No, you don't," I said. I was nearly shaking with exhaustion.

"I do. I'm sorry, Ursula." He held out his hand, again.

I wrestled the lock free and coiled it around the seat post, then shook his hand. "I'm so glad it worked out." I tried to pull my gloved hand away, but he held it. My arm tingled up to the elbow.

"What is it? What's the matter?"

"Nothing. It's just been a long day." I stood looking at my hand in his, and felt the tears well up.

"What happened?"

89

"My friend—" I shook my head.

"Kaia?"

"No. The other one."

He gave a small laugh. "Are there only two?"

I smiled. "Yes."

He squeezed my hand once and let it go. "Not anymore."

I sniffed. "Thanks. I have to go now. Tell Robbie to come home."

"Always worried about everyone else."

I backed my bike out of the rack and set my helmet on my head. There was no way to look cool in a helmet. Might as well own it. "Goodnight."

He laughed. "Goodnight."

After I checked for traffic, I pulled onto the street. I only looked back once, but he was still there, watching me.

Chapter Ten

School felt wrong without Livvie. Or, maybe, it was the drama. Most of the students polarized to my side, condemning Livvie's theft and publication of my sketches as "so wrong". A few insisted everyone needed to lighten up and take the posters for what they must have been—a joke. After all, it was common knowledge that we were "Livvie and Ursula." Best friends.

And a still smaller few acted as gossips, spreading the heinous rumor that I had somehow betrayed Liv, and that she'd planned the ultimate revenge.

At least, that's what Ella told me when we both happened to be in the restroom before school again. I listened with what I considered to be heroic patience. Livvie. My Livvie. What was she doing today? My heart ached that I had played any role in her suspension, even victim.

When I'd gotten home from Wenzinger's last night, I was too tired to hold the tears back any longer. Mom and Dad sent Leo to his room (where he no doubt laid on the floor, his ear pressed against the floor vent to eavesdrop) and I told them everything.

"Livvie Lou has gone off the rails," Dad said.

"Give it some time," urged Mom.

"I have been," I wailed. I wanted to put some blame on the two of them; they knew more about what was happening than I did. They should have told me everything from the start so I could have been more prepared.

"You two don't have to stay friends—" Mom held up one hand as I opened my mouth to protest. "But if you can stick it out, I think you'll have an even stronger friendship that's sweeter for you both."

So all day, I clung to the idea that on the other side of this dumpster fire was beauty.

Alex was already at the computer, twirling his chewed-up pen in the fingers of his left hand. He was scrolling through an article and barely noticed me as I stashed my stuff beneath the desk. I pulled my sketchbook out—a fresh, new one. The half-filled one Livvie had "borrowed" was safely at home.

He swiveled in his chair. "Missed you in the library at lunch," I told him.

"I had a little—and I mean a *little*—editing to do." He pointed at the screen.

It was my article. I knelt next to him and he scrolled through it, showing me where he'd changed a punctuation mark here, or switched sentences around there. Of course, there were tons of spelling mistakes. Spelling was my weakness. I clutched the edge of the desk while waves of embarrassment washed over me.

"If I'm not imagining it," he said, leaning back, "between Frankenstein's monster and the teacher, I see Livvie. The whole thing represents you and Livvie."

I bowed my head. "Sorry. I told you I'm not a reporter."

"Ursula, it's fantastic. I just meant that you're writing from your heart. I only see Livvie 'cause I know what you've been through this week with her. Everyone else who reads it will only feel your conviction, and know that you really believe what you're saying. That without forgiveness, nothing can be right again.

Forgiveness unmasks the monster."

"Oh. Is all that in there?"

He laughed to himself and shook his head. "You're welcome. You're a great writer, you know that? I'm a little jealous."

"Thank you. But you're being nice to me again."

He shrugged. "It's still late; I wanted it days ago, remember?"

"Better." I stood and stretched to my tiptoes then went back to my desk.

"I also changed a couple of descriptions so readers wouldn't suspect you have a big crush on Frankenstein's monster."

I faltered. Not much, but I knew he saw it. I looked up from the smooth blankness of my sketchbook page, feeling a little panicked that Alex knew. It shouldn't matter; it was none of his business. But it did matter. "He's not a believer. So I *don't* have a big crush on him."

"Hm. That's rough. Sometimes you can't help who you fall for," he said, and swiveled back to face the screen.

*   *   *   *   *

I got home and hung my coat on the hook on the wall. There was a sniff from the living room. I paused, then peeked through the doorway. Livvie was huddled in the armchair, cocooned in my favorite fuzzy blanket. Our cat, Punky, was curled on her lap and blinked smugly at me.

"Liv!" I slung my bag onto the couch and perched on the arm closest to her.

"Your mom let me in before she left to get Leo." She wiped the corner of her eye with the blanket.

"How are you?"

93

"Me?! How are *you*?"

I shrugged. "I'm fine."

"I was so horrible to you. Then you and Kaia made that movie for me."

I grinned. "I haven't seen it yet."

She pointed to the entertainment center. A DVD sleeve was resting on top of the player. "I brought it over to show your mom."

I turned on the tv and pressed play. My illustrations came to life on the screen. Kaia had done a great job finishing the slides and making the disc. Her laptop was newer than Buzzy, and she could do it way faster.

It was a short movie, but had taken hours to draw. I'd illustrated the three of us in several different locations around Jewel Valley, our school, and Wenzingers. Finally, at the end, the three little friends did a jig beneath a starry sky with a comet blazing overhead. I couldn't resist drawing the constellation Ursa Major, and pointed it out to Liv. Kaia had narrated it all with a poem. It probably took her, like, fifteen minutes to come up with the words. She was amazing like that.

"It's pretty ridiculous," I conceded, watching the final scene.

"I love it."

I sank onto the couch.

"Urs, I'm so, so sorry. I don't even have a good excuse. I was just really mad at you for siccing your mom on me. But," she shook her head vehemently, "I wasn't really even mad at you, I was just mad at me for needing help."

"Why?"

"I don't know. I'm mad that you have things I want. You have parents who get along, you're this incredible artist, you already have plans for college. All that stuff. Plus, you're talking to a cute guy who's probably going to start taking all your time. Then there

94

won't be any time left over for me. I got scared. I thought if everyone's going to leave me, I might as well leave you first."

"We're not going to leave you."

"Yes, you will. You have to if you want to go to art school." She gave me a knowing look. "And I know that's your dream. I wouldn't want you to stay if it meant giving it up."

"Liv, we'll always be friends. No matter where we live."

"I hope so. But I get so afraid sometimes. I know I should be able to handle it." She twisted her hands in the blanket.

"You don't have to handle anything by yourself. We don't want you to. So much is changing, but we're all here with you."

"I know, I know." Livvie took a deep breath. "Your mom talked to my mom the other night, and she got me in to see this friend of hers, a therapist. She's great, actually. I feel a little better, already, and today was only the first time I talked to her. I'm going to go every week for a while. So I guess I'm officially crazy."

"You're not crazy; you're smart."

"Whatever."

"Seriously. Smart people know when they need some help, and ask for it before the problem gets out of control."

She nodded. "That's sort of what the therapist said."

I jumped up and hugged Livvie, sending Punky skittering in a cloud of fur. "I'm so, so glad to see you."

"Me, too. How's it going with the Frankenstein mystery?"

I let her go. "Solved."

"No way! What happened?"

"Here, tell me what you think." I pulled out my phone and quickly emailed the article to Livvie, who read it on her phone.

As she read, her eyes shone, but the tears didn't spill over. Finally, she dropped the phone in her lap. "You wrote this? It's incredible!"

"Thanks, but I had a lot of help," I said, and shrugged.

"So, this teacher seems fantastic."

"She's … " I searched for a word, then echoed Livvie, " … incredible." I filled her in on the rest of the story, what I'd left out of the article about Matt and Robbie. "I'm waiting to hear from one of them how it went today. I'm dying to hear, actually."

"You should give him a call," she said, flipping the blanket off of her. "I'll go back home. I'm grounded anyway."

"No, stay for dinner," I said. "I feel like I haven't seen you for twenty years."

We fell into a giggling fit at the idea. "Twenty years!" she said, gasping.

I grew serious. "One day, we'll be able to say we've been friends for twenty years."

"You'll give up on me by then," she said quietly.

"Never. Neither of us will."

"Besides, you'll probably be living some place exotic." She sighed. "Northwestern. Not gonna lie, I kind of hate that place."

"It's not that far. Besides, when either of us leave Jewel Valley, distance won't matter."

Livvie slipped on her coat and promised to come over the next day. "I have to go home before my mom gets there and finds out I left the house while I'm grounded. Let me know what you find out about your Frankenstein," she said

"I will. Call Kaia."

"Okay," she agreed, then pulled the door shut behind her.

But the evening stretched on, and still there was no word from Matt. I watched my phone from the corner of my eye until I couldn't stand it any longer. I fired off a text.

?

96

I waited. And waited. At eleven o'clock, I crawled into bed and clicked off the lamp, then prayed until I fell asleep.

I dreamed I was at the Butler. It was nighttime, and I was pushing my way through a crowd lined up on the sidewalk. I fought and shoved until I was finally able to put my hands on the golden door handle. But inside, the lobby was empty. The sound of my shoes clicking on the marble floor echoed as I made my way to the balcony stairs. It was like I was underwater, I moved so slowly, but finally I gripped the balcony railing and leaned over.

The house below was empty except for someone in dark clothing on the stage. He turned. It was Frankenstein, or at least someone in a Frankenstein mask. I tried to run down the staircase but felt like I was struggling against a heavy weight. When I made it to the stage, he was gone. I climbed the stage and ducked behind the curtain, then slowly, so slowly, pushed open the big exit door to the back alley behind the Butler.

The alley seemed deserted, but I sensed he was there, watching me. I spun around and around. "Come out!" I called. "Come out of the dark!"

A hand landed on my shoulder from behind like a shackle. I tried to wriggle free but the hand held tight. I turned to stand face-to-face with the monster. He reached to pull off the mask.

I woke up. My feet were pinned in a twist of bedcovers, and my shoulder was wedged between the mattress and the wall. I sat up and checked the clock. Still forty-five minutes until I had to get out of bed. I tried to fall asleep, but by the time the alarm screeched, my eyes felt like I'd slept on a pillow of sand.

I moved through the day on autopilot, glad to have Livvie back but uneasy, still. After lunch I drifted into the office. "If it turns out badly," Alex said suddenly, one hand on the copier, "it's not your fault. You did everything you could do."

I gathered a stack of the warm pages from the tray of the copy machine. "What do you mean?"

He watched the display of the copier as it spat out page after page of our month's work. "You shouldn't worry about it so much," he muttered.

"I don't know why I haven't heard any news yet."

He shook his head but said nothing. We both knew why.

I held my cold fingers in the warm air blowing from the guts of the machine. Matt would have told me if Robbie had embraced the plan. But, maybe Matt thought it was none of my business. Had it ever really been my business in the first place? Was my involvement my own way of being a good friend, or had I crossed the line into nosiness?

When I looked up from the paper tray, he was gazing at me with such palpable pity and concern, I said. "This has to stop."

"What has to stop?"

"This." I wiggled my index finger at him. "You're freaking me out."

He took a step backward. "I'm freaking you out?"

"You're doing that thing, repeating everything I say but phrased as a question. Look. It's not even November, yet. If we're going to keep working together for the rest of the year, there can't be this—whatever. Tension."

He crossed his arms but said nothing.

"So let's go back to the way it used to be, where I hide from you, and you boss me around and pretend like you're so much older and grouch at me for drawing too slow, okay? Back to when things were easy."

He pushed his glasses onto his forehead and rubbed his eyes. "You think *that's* going to be easy?"

"Alex—"

He clapped his hands once, and his glasses fell neatly back to rest on his nose. "Okay. Whatever you want. But stay out of the library. That's my turf."

"Fine," I said stiffly.

"Pass me some envelopes. Thanks to your master work, we're late getting the print newsletter in the mail."

"Yes, sir. Thanks for the extension, boss."

"Enjoy it, because it's not going to happen again."

I felt a twinge of guilt, but knew it was better to deal with the awkwardness now. "Gotcha."

Chapter Eleven

After the last bell rang, Livvie walked me to the bike rack. "What are you going to do?"

I looked at the lowering sun. "I don't know. Maybe I should just butt out and leave everyone alone."

She tilted her head. "No, I don't think you should."

"Really? What changed your mind?"

"One: he's cute, right?"

I frowned. "You've never seen him. I mean, without the Frankenstein mask."

"And you've never said he wasn't cute, so there we are."

"His face is really symmetrical ... "

She face-palmed. "So weird. Is that an artistic way to say cute? Two: this Susanne? You said she was amazing?"

"Yes."

"You cleared all this up for her," she said. "And three: I need you to stay with it."

"Okay, that one I don't understand," I said, unfastening my helmet. "I thought you never wanted me involved."

She shook her head. "I didn't. But now I see how you're helping people, and it helps me. It's a good, sunny spot. You make me smile."

I sighed. "Then, I guess for the sake of number three, I need to find out what I can. You coming?"

She put her hands on her hips. "How? On your handlebars?"

"I can walk it … "

She checked the time on her phone. "Besides, Dad's probably on his way to get me, now. We're going out to dinner." She waved her hands in mock enthusiasm, but I could tell she was pleased to have a weeknight date with her dad.

"Okay, tell him I say hey," I said.

"I will. Go get 'em, girl."

The Arthur beehive was nearly empty by the time I pedaled across town. I walked my bike around the perimeter before deciding to check the parking lot. I found Susanne's beige sedan and was wondering if I should leave a note on the windshield when I heard a whistle. Susanne waved from the edge of the lot, the breeze lifting the fringed end of her scarlet scarf. When she was a few yards away, she called, "What's the word? They were both no-shows."

"I don't know," I said as Susanne drew closer. "Maybe something came up."

"You're not the only one who can do some investigating. Matt wasn't in his homeroom today—or any of his other classes."

I sagged. "I really thought this was the answer for everyone. I don't understand what went wrong."

Susanne shook her finger at me in mock scolding. "You can't control people. Sometimes you aren't going to get the neat, tidy ending you want."

I sighed. "I know. I just really thought this was right."

"People are messy." Susanne gave me a knowing look. "Go find out what happened. I'll be praying." She pulled her car keys from her purse. It looked like a new purse, I noticed. "And text me later! I want details!"

My map search results led me to the north side of Jewel Valley, where the neighborhoods were quiet, the houses were enormous, and the wide lawns were manicured. I checked the address on my phone again, then coasted up the black asphalt driveway. I gingerly rested my bike against the holly hedge, and pressed the glowing doorbell.

Steve opened the door. He had one hand on the doorknob, the other resting on his wallet, prepared to give me a couple of dollars in support of whatever school fundraiser must have brought me to his door.

"I'm Ursula," I said. "I was hoping to—" What was I hoping? It suddenly seemed very pushy of me to have come. "—to see Matt. Just for five minutes, please."

His brows lifted. "I've met you before, haven't I?"

"No, sir, but I've been at the Butler Theater several times recently."

He snapped his fingers. "Ah, that's it! Come on in. And don't call me 'sir', it makes me feel old. I'm guessing this visit is due to Matt staying home from school today?"

I flushed. "I was a little worried. I'm sorry. I should have waited to hear from him."

"No, no," Steve said. "I'm glad to see he's making friends. There for a while, I wasn't sure. Have a seat, I'll get him."

I sat on the edge of the overstuffed sofa, and twisted my fingers around the straps of my tote. Why had I come? I should have been more patient. With effort, I stayed put until I heard footsteps in the hallway. I swallowed.

Steve poked his head through the doorway. "Erma, I'm sorry, I guess he went out for a while. I didn't realize. He'll be sorry to have missed you, I'm sure." He didn't seem sorry, just vaguely disinterested.

I let my breath out and stood. "That's okay."

"Can I take a message?"

"Uh, just tell him I'll see him some other time." I rested a hand on my collarbone.

He grinned. "I suppose it's pointless to take messages anymore, what with texting and social this-and-that. You'll probably talk to him before I do, right?"

I smiled weakly. "Maybe so."

"Well, do me a favor," he said over his shoulder as he walked me out, "and tell him to take out the garbage when he gets back."

*   *   *   *   *

I rode to Wenzinger's like a moth to a flame. I tugged my coat tighter around me and squeezed between groups of people standing in line to pay. Perfect. Someone was in my favorite booth. Sighing, I walked to the booth in the corner. I dumped my stuff in the seat, then turned. Matt was the one who'd taken my usual spot. He flicked his fingers up in a brief wave. I waved back, uncertain. He jerked his head as an invitation to join him.

I scooped up my things and piled them in the seat opposite him. A moment passed before I ventured, "Do you want to tell me about it?"

He pointed to his phone resting on the table. "I guess you're Erma?"

I grimaced.

"Unless," he said, "someone matching your description, on a

bicycle, just left my uncle's house."

I flipped the paper place mat over to the blank white side. "I didn't give him a fake name."

"I know. He's sort of bad with names."

"Seems like a nice guy."

Matt nodded. "He wasn't exactly enthusiastic to bring us here to live. But he leaves us alone, for the most part." He pointed to the place mat. "What's that about?"

I shrugged. "Habit."

"Draw me something."

I glanced at him. People requested that a lot. But it was like the open-ended question, 'Tell me about yourself'. What in the universe would I draw? I always wanted them to narrow it down for me. Alex did that during our blogging brainstorming meetings. In fact, I usually had the opposite problem with him. He was so sure of his vision, I often had to talk him into expanding his ideas a little to give me room to play with the concepts.

But Matt would never open up that much with me. "Okay," I said.

He watched me unzip my pencil pouch and dig for my black pen. When I'd put the first lines down, he said, "I keep wondering why you're so interested. Why would someone who doesn't know us try to help? Why take the time?"

I put the thick black lines on the white paper. "I have trouble minding my own business sometimes."

"Is that the only reason, really?"

"I'm sorry if I caused problems. Seriously." I let my eyes dart around the diner as I drew, absorbing the scene and putting it down on paper. It was like a sedative. The stress I'd felt all day was melting. "I just wanted to do the right thing."

He pressed again. "So, is that your only motivation—the right thing?"

My pen paused above the paper. "Shouldn't it be?"

"Don't people matter as much as the right thing? Do you ever put people first?"

I focused on the ink, the paper. "I think that to do the right thing *is* to put people first."

He shrugged. "Sure, maybe in an all-of-mankind sort of a way, but what about individuals?"

I pulled the pen across the paper, crossing over lines I'd already made. "You don't trust me? You think I have other motives?"

"Robbie's in jail."

I stared at him. "How?!"

He looked out the window. "Back home."

"I'm so sorry."

He took a deep breath. "He … was running out of money. So he hit up a store." He shook his head. "This little corner store close to our grandma's house. And they caught him."

I didn't know what else I could say. I looked down at the place mat. There was a growing black dot where I'd let the tip of the pen rest in one spot for too long. I put the cap on it.

"No, keep drawing," Matt said, rubbing his face. "It's relaxing."

"For me, too." I studied the paper, then started again. "How long will he be in jail?"

"Gramma's going to bail him out tomorrow. Then he'll have a trial next month. Could be a while this time."

"I'm sorry," I said again. "I can't imagine what I'd do if my brother was in trouble."

"You have a brother?"

I nodded. "He's— " I was going to say he was annoying, but I pictured him in an orange jumpsuit, surrounded by strangers, some very bad. "He's ten."

Matt watched me add details to the drawing. Then I spun it

around and pushed it toward him. "Done. No more lines."

He studied the picture of the diner: the soda fountain and bar and stools, the hanging light fixtures, the jukebox, the tall booths. "This is great."

"Thanks," I said, feeling the weird twist in my stomach the way I always did when anyone looked at my drawings.

"So, I guess you're right," he said suddenly. "People don't change."

I folded my hands on the table. "We can change," I said, very gently. "I just think we need a reason bigger than ourselves to make the jump. It's too hard to do it alone."

"Isn't family a big enough reason?" he asked, and his voice was edged with bitterness. "I've made plenty of changes for him."

A bubble of laughter rose up from the soda bar. Matt glanced over his shoulder at the happy group, rocking on their stools, their heads thrown back. He turned back to me. "I don't know what to do now. I was pretty sure this wouldn't work for us. Jewel Valley. But then there was the Butler, and Steve turned out to be alright." He tore little pieces off the edge of his napkin. "Still. Robbie wasn't really into it, and, you know, I thought we'd be here for a year, tops. Just long enough for him to get his diploma. Then he'd move on, and I guess I just assumed I'd go with him. We never talked about it. It was just understood. At least to me."

Molly brought a hot chocolate. She set it on the table, winked at me, and kept moving. I pulled it toward me and wrapped my chilled hands around the ceramic. "Do you think that's why you like theater and film?"

"What do you mean?"

I gripped the mug. "I mean, you're always adapting, moving, changing. It helps to be a good actor, doesn't it?"

"My whole life," he muttered. "I should be good at it by now."

The group at the counter laughed again, this time loud enough

106

to rattle the sugar jar on the table. Matt stole another look toward the bar, then jerked a thumb at them. "They're getting to me, partly because I'm jealous."

"Because they're happy?"

He nodded. "You and the English teacher got my hopes up. I actually thought Robbie would agree to do the extra work. Then, maybe I could stay, graduate from Arthur, do theater, be in a group like *that*, for once." He eyed the loud crowd with open envy now.

"Why can't you still?"

"Robbie." He shook his head. "Always Robbie. I can't stay here while he's back home with Gramma. He'll probably lose his trial and go to jail for—" he couldn't finish the sentence, so he skipped to the next one. "I need to be with him while I can. And help Gramma out."

I took a sip of hot chocolate. It didn't seem fair for him to have to change his plans and leave. But, I pictured Leo in trouble again, and imagined how torn he must have felt.

"I spent all morning mad at you," he said.

"I'm sorry."

He shook his head again. "Don't be. It's my own stupid fault. I knew he wouldn't go to tutoring. He would never do something like that for me. And that's why I was mad. You tried to tell me he would never change, and I didn't believe you."

"I didn't say never."

"You said he couldn't do it without religion."

"It's not religion. This is a ... relationship." I tapped my heart.

He eyed me warily. "Is this the sales pitch?"

I sighed. "I'm just telling you what helps me. If I really, really believe something is true and would help you, but I don't tell you about it, that would make me a—monster—right?"

He was unconvinced. "I don't like it when people try to push their views on others."

I held up my hands. "Not pushing. Just explaining."

"You're talking about God, the Frankenstein movie's about God, Susanne was pretty clearly implying it, my gramma's talking about God, even Aunt Becky's been dropping little God hints lately. Seriously, I feel like I'm surrounded."

I shrugged. "Me, too. Makes me feel safe. Loved."

"Makes me feel paranoid."

I smiled, and he smiled back.

"Glad to see you think it's funny," he said.

"It's a little funny."

He grew serious again. "Actually, I was sort of hoping you would tell me to stay."

I bowed my head. "You have to do what you think is right."

He flopped back heavily in the seat. "There it is again. You're so sure about right and wrong, and doing the right thing. How do you know there *is* a right thing? Tell me what it is."

"I know how this sounds, since I've been snooping around ever since we met, but, really, it's your decision. You said you never get to have a say in it, right? This is your chance."

He leaned forward. "Give me a reason to stay. They'll let me pick. Gramma, Becky, Steve—they leave it up to me."

I tilted my head. "I'm sixteen. We just talked about our different beliefs. Why would you trust what I say?"

"Because," he said, "it feels like the right thing to do."

My phone buzzed. Mom.

About to start home?

I showed the screen to Matt. "I have to go."

He nodded, and peeled some ones from his wallet, leaving them beneath the napkin holder. He carefully rolled up the place mat and slid it into his pocket, then stood. "I'll walk you home. I'm not ready to go back to Steve and Becky's."

I texted Mom back.

Leaving Wenzinger's. Friend walking me.

Good. Be careful.

He pushed my bike, and I jammed my hands in my coat pockets to keep them warm. The sky was a dull orange at the horizon, and was spitting snow. The small flakes were dry, and they melted a few seconds after landing on the sidewalk and grass. I pulled my scarf higher on my neck and flipped my hood up. We were quiet as we walked toward Bluebird Street. "Are you praying?" he asked suddenly. His voice sounded strange in the quiet air, muffled by my hood but close.

I nodded. "I am a little."

"Thanks," he murmured. "You're kind of weird, you know?"

"I've been told."

"Stay that way," he said, and I realized he was going back home to the city. The sadness hit hard, and took me off guard. I walked on, struggling to keep my resolve. I knew a word, a look, would change his mind. It would be reckless, but I could have a little more time with him. And it sounded like Jewel Valley would be the best place for him. He could have some peace, unlike the upheaval of always following Robbie.

I glanced at him and watched how the snow beaded on his hair and shoulders. What would be the point of going back to the city, when by his own admission, he felt surrounded by God's conviction here? Shouldn't I try to keep him here? All the advice, all the words of teachers and parents came flooding back to me at once, like a crushing tidal wave of common sense. I knew I couldn't lead him on with false hope.

As we reached my house, we slowed. I saw Mom peek from the living room window. Then the curtain fell back into place, and the porch light flicked on. "Come inside?" I asked.

He smiled and shook his head. It would only introduce a new cast of characters for him to leave.

"I know it will be okay," I said. "But you'll stay in touch anyway, won't you?"

"I will." He let me take the handlebar, then extended his hand again.

"Good luck," I said, and took his hand. He held mine in both of his for a long moment, then leaned forward and kissed my cheek.

"See you later," he said.

I watched him walk to the end of the block, turn the corner, and disappear.

Chapter Twelve

"She's bummed because her Frankenstein's leaving." Livvie paused, eyes narrowing. "That's a sentence I never expected to say ... "

I smiled, but just a small smile. She was right; I *was* bummed and couldn't seem to shake it. For the last two days, I'd run through the Farewell-Matt scene over and over, prayed, worried, cried once or twice, but I still felt stuck in a brain fog. True, I had his number and could text anytime, but I had to admit I still didn't know him very well. I guess we could text about the Frankenstein movie, but not much else.

"Write it down," Alex said. He rolled his drink bottle between his hands. "You might never say that again. Man, it would make a great headline, though, wouldn't it?"

"Nerd," Livvie mumbled. He shot her a look of fake hurt.

But Kaia didn't say anything. I could tell that all of her cells were aimed in Blake's direction. He sat at a lunch table with the other basketball players, oblivious to her attention. How many Fridays had she been hoping for a look or sign from Blake before I'd noticed? I didn't tell anyone, not even Livvie. Poor Kaia. Poor Matt. Poor all of us. Why did it have to be so hard?

"It's just a big letdown," I complained. "I thought things would turn out okay, but it all went off the edge and crashed." I sighed. "I guess I got my hopes up too soon."

"Are we talking about Frankie—I mean, Matt—or the teacher's purse now? What hopes? What crash?" Livvie offered me the rest of her baggie of fruit snacks, but I shook my head.

"I don't know." I didn't want to admit it, but I *did* have hopes for Matt. I mean, they were tiny hopes. Hope buds. But now that he moved across the state to live with his grandma, I could feel my tiny hopes deflating.

What did I think would happen? Would all of our differences have dissolved if Robbie had stayed, gone to tutoring, and graduated? I had to admit that we probably would have discovered even more differences. But still … it was kind of fun to hang out with him. I missed meeting him at Wenzinger's. I even missed the challenge of trying to pry words out of him.

It definitely didn't seem fair, the way things turned out. I had to wonder about the purpose of it all. Why should Matt have to pay for his family's choices—first his mom's and now Robbie's? And what was the point of planting a difficult friendship with him if we'd never get to see it grow?

'Maybe,' a little voice suggested, 'it was so he would know there were people who could care about him and his family.'

I swallowed. I knew God always had a reason for things. I just wish He'd let me in on the secret this time.

"Hey, you should feel proud of helping," Livvie said, growing serious, especially for her. "And Kaia, too." She leaned over and gave me a quick hug. "It was amazing."

I felt Kaia refocusing on our table at the mention of her name. She nodded. "You made things better, not worse."

"You, too," I said, pushing bits of penne pasta around my plate with a bent metal fork. If I moved my food around enough, it would look like I'd eaten more than a few mouthfuls.

"I'm going to my locker. Come with?" Livvie grabbed her lunch bag and stood.

I shook my head but Kaia rose. "I'll come and stretch my legs."

'And walk past Blake,' I thought. A fly-by.

"So," Alex said when they'd left, "when are you going to write another article for the blog?"

I looked up at him. He seemed serious but sometimes it was hard to read his eyes behind his glasses. "Uhm, never? I mean, if I'm lucky."

He laughed. "No way, now that we know what a good writer you are, you're on the hook for more."

"Are you crazy? I have dyslexia, remember?"

"A lot of famous writers had dyslexia. That's what makes you a great investigative reporter. Your creativity helped you connect the dots when no one else could see the big picture. Don't get me wrong," he said, leaning a little closer over the table. I could see his eyes better then. They were actually a nice shade of green, and were lit up from whatever was on his mind. "Your spelling makes me want to throw the computer out of a high window. But you're still a writer now."

"Look, if I absolutely have to—if I really have something to say—I can write. But *you're* the writer; I'm the artist, remember?"

He leaned back and waited for the bell to ring before saying, over the sound of scraping chairs, "We make a great team."

I laughed and shook my head. The weirdness was back between us. Honestly, I was a little glad. "A great *publishing* team?"

We stood. "That, too," he said, and turned toward the office, where I envisioned him chewing on his pen and raking his hands through his hair as he tried to format the lunch menu for next week.

I let his words sink in. I could handle weirdness.

I'm the weird one.

Discussion Questions:

- Which of the schools in the book is most like your school: Arthur High, East River Christian, or Kaia's homeschool? Which school is the least like yours?

- Which character did you relate to the most?

- Ursula sometimes wished she had a different brain, but is learning to appreciate her own delightful mind. Have you ever wished you could be different? How do you appreciate your own differences?

- Ursula struggled to decide what to do, but she had a plan for when life gets confusing. She knew to pray, consider the good advice in the Bible, and to talk to her parents and principal. Do you have a plan? What can you do when you're faced with a hard decision?

- Ursula didn't think she could write an article until she was curious enough to risk trying. What's something you stepped outside your comfort zone to accomplish? Did it give you the confidence to try other new things?

- Ursula loves Jewel Valley, and likes to share her favorite places with friends. What are your favorite things about your own town?

- Ursula compared her drawings to Frankenstein's monster after they took on a life of their own. Have you ever created something that got twisted to hurt someone? How did you repair the situation?

- Ursula knew what she had to do to get accepted into Northwestern's art program. What are some things you can do now to help you achieve your future goals?

116

About the Author

Cole Smith is a teacher, speaker, and blogger at Cole Smith Writes. She's the author of the cozy mystery, *Waiting for Jacob*, and loves books, bikes, and coffee. She lives in West Virginia with her husband, their wire fox terrier, Arty, and a tailless cat named Mark.

Christian detective and algebra tutor, Rachel Joy, loves to solve problems ...

And life in Parkersburg, West Virginia, has no shortage. But when a church friend's daughter goes missing, Rachel must decide whether to search for a woman who doesn't want to be found, or to listen to the friends who know her best.

Relying on her faith in truth and logic, Rachel is hindered by a quirky newcomer who questions her ideals at every decision point. How can she uphold her duty but stay true to her beliefs? She can't calculate all the unknowns but maybe this time, the risk is worth taking.

Available now at Amazon.com

Thank you for reading!

Don't forget to leave a review online
at Amazon.com.

Your honest feedback helps others find this book
and lets me know what you'd like to read in my next
books.

And if you want to keep in touch, sign up for my free
newsletter at www.colesmithwrites.com